STALKED

ALIAS #1

LISA HUGHEY

Lisa Hughey

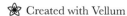 Created with Vellum

Chapter 1

Kita Kim took a direct hit across the chin. Only the heavy padding saved her from a knockout blow. Her ears rang and white stars sparkled in her vision. That was what she got for letting her mind wander, even for a moment.

Kita shook off the daze. She was trying to train Hannah Smith to defend herself. The goal was to get Hannah to engage if one of her nieces was being attacked by their father. But if she hadn't fallen into that kick, it would have lacked the force needed to really hurt her.

Hannah got in a kick to Kita's thigh. She'd probably have a bruise, but the woman hadn't used near enough force to take down a two-hundred-fifty-pound man.

"Do it again. You have to kick hard enough to hurt a guy who weighs a lot more than you do." She purposely infused her voice with perkiness, leaving out the frustration.

Hannah nodded, setting her mouth and crouching into a defensive stance. Her eyes, lost in a sea of delicate, purpling skin, glowed with anger. Her muscles trembled with rage, but her matchstick arms would be no problem for the bulk and sheer power of her abusive brother-in-law bent on attack.

Unless Kita could get Hannah ready to defend against her attacker slash abuser slash brother-in-law, he would crush this woman, just as he had crushed Hannah's sister. At least, that was what they believed. Tammy Donner had disappeared. After a cursory investigation by the local police, Frank Donner had been cleared. He insisted that his wife had run away and left him and their three daughters.

But Hannah and Kita knew the truth. Frank Donner had killed his wife. And if Kita couldn't get Hannah to defend herself and her nieces, she was worried he would kill Hannah too.

Somehow Kita had to get Hannah to embrace her rage. Whip her into a vengeance frenzy. Or at the very least, induce her to not curl up into a defensive ball.

Because Kita's boss, Jillian Larsen, had refused to help Hannah. Even though Hannah Smith and her nieces were just the type of clients usually helped by the agency Jillian had cofounded.

Adams-Larsen Inc. and Associates—publicly an exclusive PR firm—was privately a relocation specialist agency.

"We don't break the law," Jillian had said to Kita emphatically.

Because Adams-Larsen, or ALIAS, as she and her coworkers affectionately called it, skated on the edges of legality. While nothing they did was outright illegal, there were definitely blurred lines. At the end of the day, they saved people. And Kita loved being part of justice for those wronged.

Which is why this situation sucked big hairy donkey balls. Hannah Smith was in serious trouble.

Frustration bubbled in Kita's stomach. She hated when abusers picked on someone weaker. *Asshole.*

She could take down the brother-in-law with ease. But Frank Donner wasn't going after her. And Kita could only offer Hannah lessons while she wasn't on a case. If Kita received a new assignment, she'd have to cut back on training Hannah.

Kita held up her arm and rubbed her nose through the concealing face mask.

Jeez, she was ripe. The earthy odor of sweat steamed in the padded assailant suit. Her powder scent deodorant, which had worn off an hour ago, left her less than fresh. Major body odor wafted into her nose along with the unhealthy scent of Hannah Smith's fear.

Normally Kita reveled in this type of workout but Hannah's obvious discomfort hit at Kita's consciousness and her muscles were rigid with impotent frustration. Tension ratcheted up with every sobbing breath Hannah took. The threat to Hannah was real and immediate, not some faceless, nameless bogeyman, but a man who had and could kill. Even if no one but Hannah and Kita believed it. But Jillian Larsen didn't care that Kita believed Frank Donner was a killer.

"Kita." Jill had gentled her voice. "I understand your aversion to authority. It's a good part of the reason we hired you. I even understand your frustration."

Kita had rubbed at the abnormal bump on her wrist, the break that hadn't quite set properly when she was seventeen.

Jillian didn't always play by the rules either, but she couldn't understand something she'd never experienced. Kita knew in her improperly-healed, ached-when-it-rained wrist that Hannah Smith was in mortal danger.

Adams-Larsen had the means and the contacts to save Hannah and her three nieces. But they weren't going to.

"Again." Kita prepped to attack the slight woman.

The bulky padding made Kita look like the Michelin Man on steroids. Due to years of training, she could move with a fair amount of agility, probably more than Hannah's brother-in-law possessed. But Hannah needed to learn to counter the violent threat. She needed to work past her fear and get angry.

Kita rushed Hannah, roaring, trying to scare her, trying to shake her.

Within seconds Hannah leapt out of Kita's path, then twirled with a roundhouse kick to Kita's back. Kita rolled, then swept Hannah's feet out from underneath her, and she hit the padded floor with a thud. Kita jumped to her feet and leaned over her.

The woman lay on the mat, her eyes closed, her cheeks gaunt and the yellowed bruising, from the black eye before this one, apparent in the bright florescent lighting.

"You okay?"

Hannah's chest heaved. Through the entire training session she hadn't said a word. Not once had she cried out, even when Kita had struck a blow.

A single tear trailed down the side of Hannah's face and pooled in her ear. Kita's heart shattered at the defeat pulsing off this woman in waves.

"How am I ever going to do this?" Hannah's voice shook and she still hadn't opened her eyes.

Kita refused to give up.

"Right now is when you strike," Kita said fiercely. "Right now, with your heavy booted foot, you kick as hard as you can at his crotch."

Sweat poured down Kita's back, and her hair matted to her skull underneath the face mask and extra padding.

"Kick me as hard as you can," Kita demanded. "Don't hesitate. You won't hurt me." The crotch had been reinforced to protect the suit wearers, usually men, from the debilitating blows.

"You're so strong," Hannah whispered. "You don't understand how hard this is."

A heavy, gaping crater swallowed Kita's heart. Air stuck in her throat, and her lungs resisted her breath so sharply the gasp hurt. She grasped Hannah's shoulders. She hadn't always been strong. And she knew exactly how fucking hard this was for Hannah.

"You do not have to be a victim."

Hannah whimpered. Kita knew she wasn't hurting the woman, she was barely holding on to her.

"I can't do this."

"You *can*."

Kita wanted to rage at the system that let a violent offender go free to terrorize his family, the very people he should protect and keep safe.

But she knew, better than anyone, that life wasn't always fair. And the only one you could count on to protect you—was you.

For a moment she wished Marsh Adams—her friend, her mentor, the man who'd showed her these moves when she'd been facing her own demons—was here. As Jillian's partner, Marsh was the reason Kita worked for the agency. But Marsh was MIA these days, out on assignment, and no amount of wishing was going to bring him back.

"You can do this." Kita leaned forward in a lunge, holding out her hand, waiting for Hannah to grasp it so she could pull the tiny woman to her feet.

"He's going to kill me." The defeated slump of Hannah's shoulders sparked a resounding denial. No way was she going to let Hannah's asshole brother-in-law win. She'd do whatever it took to make sure Hannah and the children were safe.

"Not if I have anything to say about it."

The rumble of the employee garage door vibrated through the gym floor and the protective mats, shimmying up Kita's body to stop in the region of her heart. Adrenaline flooded her. It was the middle of the morning and as far as she knew everyone at the office was accounted for.

Except Marsh.

But ever since an incident in this building last month, the staff had been a little on edge.

Could just be someone in the field coming in for tech or ops help. Although she didn't have any appointments on her calendar. Could it be Dwayne or Victor, coming back from a relo early?

The first set of locks disengaged. Then the second door lock buzzed, the click resoundingly loud in the sudden silence of the sparring room. Hannah cowered on the floor as Kita shifted to watch the mirrors lining the wall and to observe who entered the facility.

A transparent bullet-resistant wall, made of layers of glass and polycarbonate, isolated Kita and Hannah from any threat in the hallway. The only way into the sparring room was through the password-protected entrance to the locker room on the other side of the building. The basement had been revamped to accommodate the sparring room, showers, lockers and the totally indulgent steam room.

Hannah grabbed her hand and Kita hefted her up to standing with one forceful jerk. "Again."

Kita split her attention between Hannah and the mirrors.

Hannah smoothed down the material of her yoga pants and dropped back into a defensive stance. Kita nodded in approval. *Yeah, that's it. Kick my ass.*

The steel-reinforced door opened slowly. The shadows beyond the entrance to the garage were dark and somehow ominous. Her tension ramped up as she readied to attack Hannah, while her brain shifted into higher gear, preparing to defend Hannah against danger. Which was stupid because whoever was coming through the door would have already had to go through several security checkpoints before being allowed access to the building. Adams-Larsen took their security seriously. No one who didn't belong breached the facility.

No one.

And since the shooting last month, security had been tighter than ever.

Kita's heart thumped loudly in her chest. *The ba-bump, ba-bump* a rapid percussion, as her hearing preternaturally heightened while she waited for whatever, whoever, was coming.

A silver-haired man with broad shoulders and an imperious bearing—something about his demeanor so arrogant the very air around him seemed to be holding its breath—stepped through the door. The single halogen light illuminated his face with startling clarity. She'd never officially met him, but, she knew who he was. She'd seen pictures in Marsh's office.

The judge. Marsh's father.

In the shadows behind him another man paused in the doorway. Ignoring the workout room and sparring women, the judge strode down the hallway like he owned the place.

Hannah kicked out and Kita twisted carefully to block the kick to her thigh. "You need to hit right on the knee."

Hannah nodded and crouched again.

Something in the movement of the second man drew her gaze back as he entered. He pulled the reinforced door closed behind him. The overhead halogen beam highlighted the almost blue-black of his hair and emphasized his broad shoulders. He kept his face turned away from the observation windows, staying in the shadows.

Not Marsh. It had been stupid to hope that Marsh was coming. It had been what felt like forever since he'd been in the office.

Apprehension shivered over Kita's spine. Hannah shifted so she was slightly behind Kita.

Ironic. Both the man above her and the woman behind her were hiding.

For a moment, the man paused. He had stepped into the light, head tilted down, watching the defensive tableau, his pale blue eyes piercing, glowing with intensity. Kita felt the man's regard like an almost physical caress. Her visceral reaction to the quick assessment was confusing, unwanted.

As if a rush of pheromones had drop-loaded into her system and made a beeline toward her female parts.

Her five-ten body was cocooned in the padded assailant suit, her breasts smashed and wrapped to protect from blows, and her ombre blond ponytail encased in the watch cap underneath a large padded helmet. Sex should be the last thing on her mind.

With an instant dismissal he followed the judge to the waiting elevator.

Why her hormones, which had been dormant for a very, very long time, suddenly stood up and started howling was a mystery. But the damn things were banging on the door, demanding to be let in.

Ridiculous.

"Who was that?" Hannah asked softly.

"No one we need to worry about." Kita shook the unexpected reaction to the stranger out of her head. She curled her fingers at Hannah in a "bring it on" gesture. "Kick me again."

Hannah kicked out at Kita's padded hands in a one-two-three pattern.

But there was no power behind Hannah's attack. Her moves were still timid, unsteady.

"Try to *hurt* me." Kita kept her tone firm.

But Hannah continued to be lackluster rather than aggressive.

"I just don't know if I can do this." Her shoulders slumped, her gaze dropping to the padded floor. "What if he wins?" she whispered.

"We won't let him win," Kita said fiercely. Her blood pumped in a river of anxiety but she kept her demeanor fierce.

Because she truly believed that if Hannah Smith didn't either learn to defend herself or, better yet, disappear with those kids, they would all be dead soon.

Chapter 2

A lex Saunders already hated this job.

Federal judge Robert "call me Bobby" Adams was a pain in the ass. He'd agreed to protection and then demanded a backup. A *private* backup. From everything Alex could ascertain, the judge was throwing his son a bone, tossing cash to the son's firm, Adams-Larsen Inc. and Associates. The judge insisted on hiring them as secondary security protection. A service that as far as Alex could tell, the firm was ill-equipped to provide.

Adams-Larsen was an image consulting firm. He tried to keep an open mind...although in his opinion if you lived a clean life, you shouldn't need help cleaning up your image.

So far, he'd seen a chick dressed as a giant mugger assaulting a frail woman that a strong gust of October wind would blow away. He couldn't say why he thought the mugger was a woman, except that there'd been something in her stance....

She'd been watching him and he'd had a vision of stripping away the mugger outfit to reveal what lay beneath. Her gaze had pierced the armor of his self-control and for a moment, he'd been tempted to stand by the floor-to-ceiling windows and just…watch.

Mentally he gave himself a slap. He was acting just like the guy harassing the judge. Except something hinky was definitely going on with the judge and his stalker. Alex just didn't know what. Yet.

They stopped by a receptionist's desk. The judge halted, bent to the Latina woman who guarded the inner sanctum of this business.

"Maria." The judge's voice had softened, gentled.

Ho now. What was that all about?

"Hello, Judge Adams."

"Now, darlin', I've told you to call me Bobby." He reached out to clasp one of her hands, but after she pulled back subtly, the judge patted her hand. "How are you?"

She shifted uncomfortably in her seat, her smile uneasy. "I'm doing…good."

"I'm very pleased to hear that." Judge Adams beetled his brows. "You need anything, you call me."

"Thank you, sir."

The weirdest part of the whole exchange was the way the judge acted almost fatherly toward the woman. In the two hours Alex had observed him relating to women, he hadn't once displayed this kind of behavior. And he'd watched Judge Adams interact with a *lot* of women.

"Gentlemen." A smoky contralto interrupted his thoughts. Alex turned toward the sexy voice and stopped.

She was freaking gorgeous.

Slender, stacked, and elegant. She wore a suit with a pencil skirt in a bold patriotic red, glossy lips matched her skirt and demanded attention, and a pair of heels made her legs look fantastic. She had classic Scandinavian coloring, white-blond hair, pale skin, and high cheekbones with unusual dark gray eyes.

The judge straightened. "Jillian, dear."

So this was Jillian Larsen. The judge's son's business partner. For some reason her name sounded familiar. The judge smiled and clasped Jillian Larsen around the shoulders, embracing her in a hug that went on just a little too long.

Her smile was absolutely, politely professional as she eased away. "Nice to see you again, Judge."

"Where's Marsh?"

"Marsh is on assignment right now." She was lying through her perfectly straight, unnaturally white teeth. "He sent his regrets."

"Not a problem." The judge dismissed the statement, either not knowing or not caring that she'd lied. "I had planned to request a favor from *you* in any event."

"Why don't you both come into my office." Jillian Larsen led them toward a set of tall mahogany doors. "And you can tell me all about it."

Her stride hitched for a barely perceptible moment, then she led them away from the giant desk situated in front of a wall of bookshelves and toward a more casual sitting area with wing chairs and a small sofa. She strode easily and confidently, leaving the men in her wake, while the judge stared at her butt for just a little too long.

She was young enough be to his daughter. But that didn't seem to matter to the man. He was an equal opportunity dawg. With the very bizarre exception of the receptionist.

Jillian Larsen sat in a wing chair, leaving another chair and a settee for Alex and the judge.

Quickly Judge Adams introduced Alex, only by name,

not mentioning the reason he was accompanied, then skimmed over the details of his problem.

Jillian Larsen didn't say a word as the judge glossed over the specifics of receiving very detailed emails, expertly encoded letters no less, with explicit death threats. No cut-and-paste pictures out of magazines for this guy. The US Marshals' computer guys were still trying to de-code the high-tech encryption. And they still hadn't determined where the emails originated from.

Jillian listened intently, her mouth pursed and her unusual gray eyes flat.

The judge wound up, "So you see my dear, I'm hoping that we can hire you to be an additional…pair of eyes until this nonsense stops."

Without even glancing at Alex, she demurred. "You're asking us to engage out of our area of expertise, Judge. You are not our typical agency client." She pulled out a smartphone and started thumbing through her contacts. "I can recommend several good security—"

"Jillian. Cut the horseshit." The judge's affable, good-old-boy demeanor had been replaced by the guy who'd managed to survive the Congressional vetting process unscathed and made difficult decisions to send traitors and high-level criminals to federal prison for life. "I need you to make this happen."

Alex was pretty sure there was a threat in Judge Adams's words but damned if he could figure out that underlying warning.

"You're in a precarious position as it is after the debacle last month with the FBI."

Maybe that was why her name sounded familiar. Memories finally clicked. A prominent Russian businessman with shady connections had been killed in a shootout right here at Adams-Larsen. The story in the press was that the Russian had a love interest in DC and had entered the country illegally. Something had gone awry and he'd taken a hostage. Congress was set to hold private hearings on the situation, wanting to know how the man got into the country and why he ended up dead. Alex had thought there was a whole hell of a lot of logistical things left out of that story.

"It would be embarrassing if you ended up with more negative press. Not great for a...PR agency."

Mentally Alex perked up. Forget the prior veiled warning, the judge had just very clearly and overtly bullied Jillian Larsen, his son's business partner. Although Alex still had no idea what the judge was talking about.

Jillian blinked, never once losing her composure. "With Bliss and Rissa mostly on the West Coast these days, I'm shorthanded right now."

"You'll do."

Denial in her gaze was swift but her comeback was smooth and unhurried. "I'm sorry but I'm needed here at the moment. Perhaps Dwayne."

"Need a woman." The judge was shaking his head. "She can pose as my personal aide."

Finally the reason they were here clicked in Alex's brain. The judge didn't want an additional bodyguard, he wanted a playmate. Or he wanted a bodyguard who looked like a playmate.

"Ms. Larsen, perhaps it would ease your mind to know that the US Marshals will be running point on Judge Adams's case and he will be under their protection."

"That would be you?" she asked coolly.

Alex nodded. "Yes, ma'am."

Her eyes went flat again, almost as if his being a deputy

marshal worked against him. Alex could practically see her brain synapses firing as she considered then rejected options. But she didn't shut the judge down. Did that mean she didn't trust the US Marshals? The United States Marshals office was the best personal protection security in the world. Certainly head and shoulders above some Beltway spin doctors who were so bad at PR they were going to be part of a congressional hearing.

This detail was a freaking train wreck.

But on his last job, after loudly protesting the authenticity and suitability of the US Marshal's witness he'd been charged with protecting, Alex had received an official reprimand from HR. It didn't matter that his instincts had been right on target. The fucking idiot had violated the terms of WitSec within a week of being relocated, and in another week he'd been dead.

Killed by the very people he was supposed to be hiding from.

Alex had a bad feeling about this job. But the ding in his personnel file didn't give a shit, and he could not afford to fuck up this assignment.

The immediate consequence of speaking up on his last case had been a transfer to the Judicial Protection branch of the Marshals, and the protection of one ornery Judge Robert "call me Bobby" Adams.

Right away the judge had put him in an awkward position by requesting the addition of an Adams-Larsen employee. But Alex's new boss told him to do whatever the judge wanted to keep him happy. Having additional backup outside the assigned Marshals—namely *him* and his partner, Shep—was highly unusual.

"I may have one person." She was so reluctant that Alex couldn't imagine her choice would be acceptable.

"Well, go get her," the judge ordered.

Jillian Larsen moved elegantly, crossing her legs, and pressed a button on her cell phone, turning it into a two-way comm system. "Maria, can you page Kita for me?"

The judge glanced at his diamond-rimmed, 14-carat gold Rolex. "I've got an important pretrial meeting in an hour."

Alex was an expert at reading people. Jillian Larsen wanted desperately to tell Judge Adams to go to hell, but she pasted a very polite smile on her lips and held back the harsh words.

"Maria, have her come up right away."

Alex made a mental note to check into the background of the employees of this agency. He hadn't had a chance to do more than find out they did image consulting since Judge Adams dropped this bomb on him.

"But, Jill." They could all hear the hesitation in her assistant's voice. "She's in the sparring room."

"Right. Away."

"Okay." *You asked for it* was implicitly implied in the receptionist's dubious tone.

Chapter 3

K ita rushed up the stairs. Was something wrong with Marsh? She couldn't believe that thought hadn't occurred to her when the judge walked in.

They needed to see her right away.

She'd removed the padded assailant suit, stripped down to a tight wicking sleeveless top and a pair of skimpy spandex shorts. She'd tugged on a pair of running shoes and splashed water on her face and skimmed over her pony. The temp inside the assailant suit got damn hot and her face felt like she'd sat in the sun at a Nationals game in the dead of summer. She also smelled a little funky and the quick spritz of Dwayne's Axe didn't really mask the odor. She'd have preferred a cold shower. But Jillian had said, "Right away."

Kita burst into the reception area. "Everything okay? Something wrong with Marsh?"

"Not as far as I know," Maria Torres said softly. She was still finding her confidence. She'd been abducted as a teenager and spent eight years in a solitary prison before she'd managed to escape. Kita couldn't even imagine the fortitude it had taken for her to not crumble up and wither away. But she hadn't. And slowly but surely Maria was coming out of her shell and growing into the woman she was meant to be.

Relief washed over Kita.

"When you ask for *right away*, this is what you get, stinky and sweaty." Kita grinned.

"Apparently they couldn't wait for you." Maria rolled her eyes and Kita loved that little bit of 'tude. "Go on in."

She strode into Jillian Larsen's office, then felt as if she'd walked into an alternative dimension.

Three people, elegantly dressed, sipping beverages out of delicate china cups, turned at the same time as if choreographed. They were having a tea party and she'd just crashed it.

"You wanted to see me." *Right away.* They sure hadn't given her time to clean up.

"Kita, thanks for coming so quickly." Jillian put down her cup, the clatter of china loud in the suddenly silent room.

In her St. John suit and matching pumps, with her perfectly smooth blond hair and expertly applied makeup, Jill was the epitome of polished and poised. Kita was the unkempt homeless girl compared to Jillian's high society princess.

Both men rose to their feet. If she hadn't been distracted by the sheer power of the man to her right she might have been amused at their old-fashioned gesture.

Immediately her gaze went to the unknown man. Up close his presence was even more compelling. Blue-black hair, a leanly chiseled, uncompromising face, and the stoic expression in his reserved pale blue eyes captivated her.

Like the magnetic pull of the moon, she couldn't stop

staring at him. She was drawn to him. Power. He'd exuded it merely sitting in the effeminate chair.

His shoulders were broad, and although his button-down cotton shirt was just a little too loose to reveal the muscles beneath, she sensed his strength. And she wondered again who he was and what he wanted with her.

She knew what she wanted with him.

Hot sweaty sex. Early morning sex, late morning sex, afternoon sex, "hi, honey I'm home, holy-shit-can't-make-it-to-the-bedroom-do-it-against-the-wall" sex.

Bad Kita. Not the time to be thinking about sex. She flushed, her body going hot and weak. Damn it.

As if by moving her gaze she could get rid of the potentially embarrassing attraction that swamped her body, Kita shifted her attention to the judge.

She'd known Marsh since middle school. Had even lived with him and his mom for the last half of her senior year of high school but she'd never met Marsh's father. She knew him through his actions though. The judge had pretty much ignored Marsh until his profession was of use to him. Judge Adams was a mover and a shaker in DC political circles. He was also the kind of user that made her skin crawl.

He was buffed and polished. He clearly visited his esthetician once a week, tanned and near glowing, like freaking neon in a pale yellow button-down shirt and khakis. She'd bet her brand new custom-designed Trek Fuel-Ex mountain bike he got his fingernails manicured.

Instinctively, Kita curled her fingers under to hide her unpolished nails.

"Oh, she won't do at all."

Excuse me?

"Now, Judge." Jillian placed her fingers over the judge's forearm, naturally drawing his attention back to her. *Nice move, Jill.* "Kita has been training. You didn't give her time to get cleaned up."

Kita wanted to protest. This *was* her. A little sweatier, a little redder in the face maybe, but what you saw was what you got. And she'd be damned if she apologized for it. She was kick-ass great at her job. But she waited patiently to see what Jillian would do next. And tried to figure out what the heck the judge needed her for.

Judge Adams surveyed her up and down, frowning with concentration. "I'm not sure...."

The entire time the judge was examining Kita like a horse at auction, she was preternaturally aware of the man to her side. Since when did you need to assess your training expert for appearance?

The mystery man with the judge hadn't said a single word. He finally spoke. "Maybe you should let her decide if she wants the job." The deep rumble shivered through her body, slipping through her bloodstream like an addictive drug. God, even his voice was sexy.

Her embarrassment mounted at her body's physical reaction to the timbre of his voice. Fortunately, no one else knew she'd had such a sexual response, and she'd damn well better keep it that way.

Time to speak up. She wasn't a doormat and she wasn't a victim. Not anymore. "What job?"

For a moment, no one spoke.

Jillian finally answered. "The judge has a...security issue."

"Why not use Jake?" Except Jake was on their current hush-hush relo and not due back until next week.

"Not an option," Jill confirmed.

"Dwayne?"

"Not the correct set of...attributes."

"What's the security issue?" Did they want her comp skills? Or her self-defense skills?

"He's been getting death threats," the stranger offered.

The judge blustered, "The usual threats a man in my position acquires."

Could the judge be getting threats from the exposure of the rotten, amoral politician who'd imprisoned Maria for years? Perhaps the judge's role in identifying and apprehending the dirty fucker had been discovered.

"He needs protection," Jill said.

Kita pondered the judge's brush-off sentence. *The usual* death threats.

Not so usual if they were coming to the Adams-Larsen agency for help. Although physical protection was outside their normal duties, Kita wasn't about to say that out loud. She held her words, waiting and assessing.

"The judge has *requested* our help." Jillian's lips tightened. She wasn't happy about the request. She also wasn't being very forthcoming.

The only reason Jillian would be bowing to help the judge was if he'd forced the issue. And what possible repercussions could the judge invoke on the company? To the outside world, Adams-Larsen Inc. and Associates dealt in sensitive public relations and spin.

While they did do some image consulting, the main focus of their business was helping innocent people in trouble disappear. Legally. People like the whistleblower in the Enron case. Or an abused woman. Or someone falsely accused in the social media-verse. Some of the things happening on Twitter and Facebook were downright terrifying. Or someone who would not be well served by entering the Federal Witness Protection Program, a program designed for criminals testifying against other criminals. But very few people knew this.

Jillian gestured to the teapot. "Would you like a drink while we discuss this?"

Now Kita was really confused. Jillian was usually very direct. And Kita was still a sweaty mess with no place to sit.

"We don't have time for niceties." The judge dismissed Kita's comfort with a wave of his hand and then sat back down. "Let's get to it."

The stranger had kept his steady gaze on Kita the entire time. The intense observation felt nothing like the judge's condemning appraisal. She knew without a doubt that hot guy was thinking about her and sex.

Her body was thinking right back.

She hadn't had sex in forever. Too busy. Too wary. Too guarded. And frankly even though she started out aroused and on board, by the time they got to the main act she was so tense that she rarely enjoyed it anyway. Although, the way her body responded to him, he might be the exception rather than the rule.

And holy bananas, why did her mind keep returning to sex? The guy wasn't that hot. *Focus on the job, Kita.* She wanted clarification. "You want self-defense lessons?"

"Backup protection," the stranger said as if the concept were distasteful. His gaze turned appraising but not in a blatantly sexual way. It was Kita's problem that her body didn't seem to notice. She didn't work security. She didn't do fieldwork at all. She did computer work and social media seeding. She combed data to make sure that once their client was in their new location, she could misdirect anyone trying to track them. She helped them set up new accounts and trained them on how to keep from giving away their location. The other component of her job was to train their clients in self-defense.

Her job had never been protection. So why would this guy, and the judge, think she was the proper person for the judge's request?

Kita's curiosity finally got the better of her. "And you are?"

"Alex Saunders. US Deputy Marshal." He held out his hand.

She took the shake hesitantly. He didn't linger, his rough palm slid against hers and a shiver whispered over her spine. What had he said?

Marshal? So apparently the Marshal's service protected federal judges from threats.

She was damn sure this US Marshal wouldn't approve of the work they did here at the agency.

"And you need backup?" She raised the brow over her right eye, the words coming out far more provocatively, and challenging, than she anticipated.

Something hot and dangerous flared in Alex Saunders's ice blue eyes. "The judge wants it."

And what the judge wants the judge gets? According to Marsh it had always been that way.

"Jillian, are you sure this is all you have?" The judge was frowning at Kita as if she'd pooped on the ancient Persian carpet. "I need someone to pose as my aide and... companion. But no one would believe I'd hire her."

His words and tone were so derogatory that Kita couldn't speak. He'd just insulted her...to her face no less. "I assure you, Judge." Jillian's demeanor was all professional now. "Kita can look the part of your aide. You've caught her at a disadvantage."

"Perhaps we should review this."

It would be fine if she never saw this asshat again. She couldn't believe what a jerk he was. How had Marsh Adams, an extraordinary and gentle man, been spawned from this chauvinist pig? Now she understood why Marsh had never introduced her to his father on the rare occasion he'd visited Marsh as a teenager. While the omission had stung back then, now she completely got it.

"I don't have anyone else," Jillian said firmly.

"Judge," Alex started.

"Call me Bobby."

Kita shuddered at the affable, hearty, smarmy smile.

Alex Saunders continued, "Perhaps since this…agency is shorthanded, it would be best to only use the government-supplied, highly trained Marshals to protect you."

Oops. Wrong thing to say. Clearly. The judge stiffened.

If she was annoyed, the judge was a million times more upset. His face reddened, pushing the small broken blood vessels in his nose and cheeks to the surface. The flush spread all the way up to his thick silver hairline. "I want additional backup to be provided by Adams-Larsen."

Kita definitely heard a threat in that statement.

There was something else going on. Alex Saunders didn't want her working with him. Or anyone else from Adams-Larsen? That remained to be seen.

But based on the judge's reaction, if Alex Saunders didn't toe the line he'd be the one out and then Kita would be watching Judge Dickhead all by herself.

There was the slightest of hesitations. So slight, Kita wasn't sure if anyone but her noticed. The skin around Saunders's pale eyes tightened. He hated the idea.

But as if he flipped a mental switch, he dipped his chin deferentially. "Yes, sir."

"That's better." The judge nodded. "I guess I'll give you a try."

Kita's stomach rolled, the rice and kimchi she'd had for breakfast threatening to come back up.

Alex Saunders said forcefully, "I'm the lead on security."

"Of course," Kita answered. She gave Jillian a pointed look. They would be talking about this change of affairs later. In private.

Jill dipped her chin in understanding. Because if Kita was doing this, she was getting something out of it.

The judge waved off Saunders.

"I have a fundraising event tonight." Judge Adams had clearly moved on. "You'll need to dress appropriately. Consider it a rehearsal. If things go well, then I guess you'll do."

Chapter 4

A lex had completely lost control of this assignment.
Fuck.

His inconvenient attraction aside, what was the judge thinking? Before he could offer a protest, quietly, discreetly, about using Kita Kim, his cell rang. His boss. He held up a finger, knowing that gesture was going to piss off everyone in the room. "Excuse me a moment."

"Saunders." He paced to the outer edges of the stuffy, formal room, trying to keep his voice low.

"We've got actionable intelligence," Deanna Womack barked.

"Name, location." Motive?

For some reason his gaze was continually drawn back to Kita Kim. Even though he never lost his focus on the information his boss was relaying, her essence was like a beacon. Once his boss finished, Alex said, "You want me and Gaffney to check it out?"

Kita Kim swaggered over to him, all confident and cocksure, even with the disadvantage of being in sweaty spandex and a tight wicking top. "You have something?"

He put his hand over the mouthpiece of his cell. "Give me a sec."

She edged closer, so close she invaded his senses. Woman and sweat and underlaid with some delicate citrus and spice scent that completely contradicted her aggressive personality.

His boss was jabbering in his ear about important protectees and keeping the judge happy and yet still guaranteeing his safety. She finished with, "Take Jill's operative with you."

Operative. A strange word for a PR person but whatever. His initial instinctive reaction was to argue. Unfortunately, he wasn't in any position to disagree with his boss. Dammit.

"Ten-four."

Kita poked her finger into his pectorals. "You're taking me with you."

She'd tilted her chin up, her nearly black eyes sultry, and blasted his thoughts to a place that was far from an appropriate reaction to a coworker. Dammit, he needed to get his raging hormones under control.

Something about her, certainly not her attitude, had caused his body to react in a most innately visceral and unexpectedly sexual manner. Which was insane on several levels. But damn, his body had stood up and taken notice the moment she'd come into the room. Despite the fact that she was disheveled, sweaty, and clearly not his type.

Jillian Larsen eyed him shrewdly. "You have a lead."

"Yes."

Alex studied her. While he could appreciate her attributes, she left him cold. As Kita Kim swaggered into his personal space, he realized, amused at himself, he was more turned on by the woman who had been wrapped up in a thick insulated suit and smelled like it, than the sophisticated, urbane Larsen. What did that say about him?

He'd been working too long without a break.

And he was going to have to take Kita Kim with him, at least for right now. Maybe he could still luck out and she wouldn't pass the judge's sexy aide/playmate test.

"Judge, you're going back to your office with Deputy Marshal Gaffney while Ms. Kim and I check out this lead."

Kita nodded, a purely satisfied smile curved her mouth.

Alex couldn't resist. "Consider it *your* audition for *me*."

Her smirk made him want to press closer, throw her off her game, muss up that supreme confidence. Which was completely unprofessional. "Not sure you can handle me."

He knew how he'd like to handle her.

Alex reverted to protocol to save himself from blurting out something completely inappropriate, "Ms. Larsen, we need to escort the judge to his car."

"Of course."

"Give me five minutes to change into something a little more professional." Kita Kim headed out the door.

This case was already too complicated. Maybe they could catch a break and it would be over before it started.

KITA WAITED for Alex Saunders to fold his large form and long legs into the front seat of her Prius.

Unassuming. Good gas mileage. Excellent for the environment. But hell on super long legs. He fit but it wasn't optimal. His expression reinforced her observation. Grumpy.

She must have imagined that smoldering look in Jill's office. "I guess you're too big."

Flirty, a little inappropriate, but guaranteed to throw the guy off.

He shot her an inscrutable look. She wanted to snicker but instead she said blandly, "Where to?"

He named an address in the outer suburbs. But didn't say anything more.

Kita peeled out of the Adams-Larsen parking lot across the back alley. "Who are we going to see?"

"Disgruntled husband of a woman the judge just sent to federal prison for violating a non-compete clause on an employment contract."

"Seems somewhat harmless."

"Except the government has been cracking down on this kind of white collar crime, and the evidence was irrefutable. She benefited by stealing client contact lists."

Kita thought for a moment. "Hardly seems passionate enough to physically threaten a sitting federal judge. What else have you got?"

"That's it."

She hummed, turning over possibilities and scenarios in her head. She might not have been field certified for the CIA but she was a hell of a strategist. She'd written briefs on interrogation analysis. But Alex Saunders didn't know that, and he likely didn't have the clearance needed to find out. So she'd allow him the lead unless she saw an opportunity. "What's our strategy going in?"

Alex Saunders lifted his eyebrows.

"I can be bad cop," she said with a particular glee. If she was going to go into the field, she wanted to have some fun.

"I'll question him."

Keep your mouth shut was implied.

"What type of intel have you got then?" She sighed. He was no fun.

Alex Saunders thumbed through the screen on his phone. "He made verbal threats at the sentencing hearing."

"Why wasn't this checked out before?" Kita frowned. He seemed like a rule-following kind of guy. And overt threats made against the judge in the courtroom seemed to be a slam dunk. Of course, nothing was ever an actual slam dunk. The nuances and intricacies of espionage situations were convoluted and complex.

"I don't know," he said grimly. "But I will find out."

They arrived at the residence of the man in question. The front yard was overgrown, weeds choking out the dead and dying annuals in the front flower bed. The grass was trimmed but the rest of the bushes and flowers had a neglected air about them.

Kita bent to finger a bright red geranium that just needed to be deadheaded for the flowers to come back. The leaves were velvety and green and well-kept.

"What are you doing?" His dress shoes clicked on the cement walkway leading up to the front door. The blue door with glass panels to each side displayed a grapevine wreath wrapped in a red, white and blue flag ribbon and festooned with faded red silk carnations.

Kita glanced around the neighborhood. Middle class, well-maintained, the kind of neighborhood that kept secrets as well as nicely manicured lawns. The cars were mid-range older models, and the suspect's home was no exception.

Although the residence certainly didn't indicate any type of imbalance in income or a status beyond the rest of the neighborhood. Not that the woman the judge sentenced couldn't have hidden her ill-gotten gains, but something definitely seemed a little off.

"Where's her money?"

Alex ignored her and knocked on the front door.

They could hear someone coming. Alex unsnapped the strap on his holster and put his hand on the grip of his government-issued weapon.

"Is that necessary?"

Kita wasn't worried. But she was very cognizant that an upstanding, middle class façade could hide evil.

"Precautionary."

"We're just talking to him."

Alex nodded shortly.

The door jerked open. A disheveled man—hair askew, at least a week of gray stubble on his chin, and clad in pajamas and a bathrobe that definitely hadn't seen a washing machine anytime lately—stared blankly at them.

No one spoke. Finally Kita said, "Mr. Gauss?"

Her question seemed to shake him out of his stupor. "Yes." His voice was gravelly, as if he hadn't spoken in a while.

She could be wrong but he didn't appear to be in any shape mentally to be threatening the judge.

"Deputy Marshal Alex Saunders." Alex shoved out his hand. "Can we ask you a few questions?"

The man turned around and shuffled toward the sofa just visible past the open door. "I have to talk to you, right?"

The weary acceptance in his rough question sparked Kita's compassion. She glanced around the living room. A fine layer of dust covered everything. A philodendron in the corner had ruffled leaves brown at the edges, and a spider plant in a stand by the front window was more transparent fronds than healthy green-and-white striped leaves.

Kita stuck her finger in the pot and jammed up against hard dirt.

"Would you prefer a lawyer present?" Alex Saunders asked. Dumb. He should have just gone for it. Mr. Gauss wasn't thinking clearly.

And if this guy had anything to do with threatening letters to the judge, she would eat her poisonous pothos.

Mr. Gauss laughed cynically. "Lawyer didn't do any good. Why pay one now?"

Kita wanted a look at the guy's computer while Alex Saunders quizzed him.

"Mr. Gauss. Would you like me to water your plants?"

He blinked, looked around as if just noticing that his houseplants were dying. "Sure?"

Saunders frowned at her.

Kita hustled into the kitchen, listening with half an ear while Alex Saunders began to interrogate the man.

Kita rummaged through the cabinets until she found a tall glass. She lifted the tap and let the water run. A desktop sat on the small desk built into the kitchen cabinet area and was covered in dust. Kita glanced in the living room, then pressed the power button.

While the laptop powered up, she filled the glass with water and bustled back into the living room. First she pinched off the dead leaves from the spider plant then slowly watered the plant, careful not to overwater.

Alex kept his focus on the man, who was becoming agitated, but she could feel her partner's censure in the tightness of his mouth. What had she done wrong?

Kita strode back into the kitchen and bent over the keyboard, checking the last time Mr. Gauss had gotten online and what kind of programs he had on his home computer.

It was a basic model probably bought on sale. She

skimmed through the directory on his hard drive. He hadn't even logged online in two weeks. There was no way this guy was the stalker.

Kita quickly powered down the computer and filled the glass once more.

She returned to the living room and tended to the philodendron with the same care she'd given the spider plant.

Mr. Gauss was ranting. "Haven't you people destroyed my life enough? My wife was innocent."

Alex Saunders was trying to placate the man but it wasn't going well. "Judge Adams has been receiving threats."

"Good." Mr. Gauss's hand trembled as he took a sip of water. "I hope he's as miserable as I am."

"It's a federal offense to threaten an officer of the court."

"Whatever. The man deserves whatever he gets. He sent my wife to prison."

For a crime it seemed clear she committed. Except where were the funds? Where was the extravagance? Kita saw no overt signs that Mrs. Gauss had skimmed client lists to benefit her new company. But even Mr. Gauss's anger was lackluster. He was not their guy.

Kita patted him on the shoulder. "If you just pinch and water once a week, your plants will stay healthy."

He blinked and smiled wanly at her. "Thank you. My wife usually takes care of the greenery." He looked around his living room as if seeing the still banded-up newspapers and the dirty plates on the coffee table for the first time.

He stood abruptly. "I didn't have anything to do with those threats. But I'd like you to leave now."

Alex Saunders shot her a dirty look. "Thank you for your time."

He quietly stormed out the door. He didn't say a word as she followed behind him.

"WHAT WAS THAT?" Alex gritted his teeth. He wasn't quite sure how he'd lost complete control of that interview.

He was trained to analyze people for a living. While of course the psychiatrists and doctors had their own analyses of potential WitSec recipients, the agents weighed in on suitability since they tended to spend more time and interact with the witnesses. And he knew what to do to assess and report on a potential witness.

He'd been surprised by her compassion toward the broken man.

Kita shrugged. Shrugged! "He isn't our guy."

She was right. "We still have to follow protocol and interview him as if he were our suspect."

"That was your job." She put the car in gear and headed back toward the center of DC. "Besides, I checked his computer log. He hadn't been online in two weeks. If he's been sending encrypted emails, he hasn't been doing it from home."

Frustration boiled inside him like a cauldron. "You... checked his computer."

"Yeah."

He noted her relaxed posture, her delicate hands loose on the wheel. As if she hadn't just broken several laws by illegally searching his computer.

"We didn't have a warrant." And shit, his voice had risen. Was she trying to get him fired?

"If I'd found anything, I would have shut it down and we could have come back with a warrant."

"With enough time for him to delete or hide the evidence."

"C'mon, Al—Deputy Saunders," Kita said. "If he'd done it, we would have found another way to prove it. Unless you completely wipe a hard drive, which *ding ding* would be a huge clue that you'd done something wrong, most deleted data can be retrieved."

"There are rules, laws in place for a reason." His heart pounded into his throat. How the hell was he supposed to work with someone who had no respect for protocol?

She laughed, the sound a light cascade of notes, that raised his blood pressure even more.

Then she patted his hand, just like she'd patted the sad and pathetic Mr. Gauss. "It all worked out."

The sexual attraction he'd kept under wraps unexpectedly zapped him. How could he be attracted to her? Yes, of course, his hormones appreciated her, but her disregard for proper procedure and her lack of respect for the rules should override any physical attraction.

But his body didn't give a shit. His dick was interested and happy to be near her.

She snatched her fingers back and kept her eye on the road. "All's well that ends well."

Alex could only hope that the judge would find her lacking as a potential companion.

Because his boss told him he had to play nice, which meant he couldn't object to her presence no matter how much he wanted to.

"Do not subvert the rules again."

"Sure, Deputy Marshal Saunders." Her voice was a low throaty purr and he thought she was poking fun at him.

She pulled up to the employee entrance to the judge's office.

Alex swung open the door and extricated himself from the little car. "Be back in two hours."

Chapter 5

A fter dropping Mr. Grumpy at the judge's office, Kita headed back to ALIAS. She was going to need hazard pay to deal with the oh-so-serious Deputy Marshal Saunders. She knocked, then opened Jill's office door.

"How did it go?" Jillian sank onto the delicate wing-back chair with the crewel embroidery, leaned her head back, and closed her eyes.

"Well, as much as the vaunted US Marshal's service has a stellar reputation, we didn't solve the case quite yet," Kita said drily.

"Oh. My. God."

Kita stalked over to the chair vacated by Alex Saunders. She had the inexplicable urge to dominate the space he'd been occupying earlier. What that said about her she had no idea. She plopped down into the upholstered chair and swore she could still smell his scent, a mix of soap and pine lingering in the air, taunting her all over again. "Jillian. What the heck is really going on?"

Jillian had that old world WASP vibe that always made

Kita hesitate to swear in front of her. It was a weird dynamic. Jillian was her boss. Jillian and Marsh had been pals when they'd worked for the US Marshals, while Kita and Marsh had been friends since middle school. Kita always felt a subtle competition for Marsh's affection between them. She was probably imagining it.

"The judge wants protection."

Screw it. "The judge is an asshole."

Jillian laughed. "No argument there."

"Why us?"

"I have no idea. But I can tell you this." Jillian straightened and looked Kita right in the eyes. "He knows what we really do. And if we don't comply, he'll out us. That threat was very clear."

Since their main focus was helping innocent people in trouble disappear, their business was extremely hush-hush and confidential. If the word got out about Adams-Larsen's true business, their clients would be in jeopardy.

"I will not let that fucker win."

Kita snorted. Just when she thought she had Jillian pegged, she went and did or said something completely out of character.

"What does Marsh say?"

Jillian pressed her lips together. What the heck?

"Jillian?"

"I haven't heard from Marsh."

"You…." Kita had just assumed he was on a top secret relocation. They'd had one or two lately so incredibly sensitive that only the bosses knew where the client was being placed. "But I thought—"

"Yeah." Jillian Larsen rubbed a hand over her forehead. Her perfect French manicure gleamed in the beam of the overhead lights. "He's AWOL. I don't know why or how. He told me he needed a little time off. I thought he meant, you know, like a weekend or something."

"Have you tried his cell?"

"Straight to voice mail."

"House?"

"Locked up tight."

"House on the Cape?"

"Empty and dusty."

"Holy shit."

"Yeah." The strain of keeping that information to herself, for the past month, holy freaking cow, surfaced in Jillian's voice.

"And you think his father has any idea?"

"No. But if we don't keep the judge happy then he might just go digging."

So Jill was in a tough spot. Kita could use this to her advantage. "How happy?"

"I need you to keep him safe and keep him off our backs and frankly away from the office. I can't lie for Marsh forever." Jillian frowned. "The judge wasn't giving us the full truth about the letters he's received. They don't assign Marshal protection for routine threats."

That's what she figured. "You have copies of the letters?"

"Alex Saunders is supposed to forward them to me so I can take a look."

Alex Saunders. Just his name sent a smattering of goose bumps across Kita's neck. Her body was still on high alert from his presence. Her core warm and gooey when she remembered his husky laugh in the heated confines of her little car.

Kita hesitated. "I'd like to trace the IP address."

Jillian squared her shoulders. "Okay. I'll analyze the letters. I'm stuck here. With Marsh gone, I can't afford to be away from the office."

So the judge had made a bid for Jillian. That made sense on several levels. It also meant Kita was going to be doing Jillian a favor. A big favor.

Jillian continued, "The judge may...come on a little strong."

"I can deal."

Jillian hesitated again. "Can you handle it if the judge gets overly aggressive?"

"I'll handle it," she snipped. Besides, the judge wasn't too impressed with her charms.

"When he sees you dressed to kill, he may change his mind," Jillian said as if she'd read Kita's thoughts.

"I'll handle him." Kita dismissed Jillian's concern. "This assignment isn't in my job description."

It was so far from her job description as to be laughable.

"I know. I can't force you to take the assignment."

But if Kita did do this.... Possibilities swirled in her brain.

"I'll make it up to you." Jillian practically begged. "But I need you to make the judge happy. The future of our business depends on his keeping his mouth shut."

Kita knew why she was going to do this. Marsh had applauded her out-of-the-box thinking on more than one occasion. She was going to out of the box Hannah Smith right out of a dangerous situation.

"Okay. I'll do it but I want something in return," Kita said grimly. "Something worth *my* while."

"What?"

"Relocate Hannah Smith and the children pro bono."

"Are you kidding me?" Jillian reared back as if Kita had advanced aggressively.

"Frank Donner is dangerous," Kita argued. "He killed her sister and got away with it. He's beating up Hannah regularly. You know at some point he'll start hitting his kids."

"They're *his* kids."

Kita knew that. It was why Jill had refused the first time around. It was why Hannah Smith was taking self-defense classes from Kita. But she wasn't responding to the self-defense training. "I know."

"That's...."

"Technically against the law."

"Kita, we already had this discussion. That would take us into an area I don't want to tread." Jillian's gaze was troubled. "Everything we do is done legally. I can't start breaking the law."

"What about Frank Donner?"

"We don't have the right to take his children away."

"Tammy Donner disappeared. Hannah knows he killed her."

"The police investigated. He was cleared," Jill shot back. "He has an airtight alibi."

"Hannah doesn't know how he did it, but she's sure he killed her sister."

Jill sighed.

"Do you really want Hannah Smith's death on your conscience?" 'Cause Kita sure as hell didn't. "What if we just relocate them for a temporary time?"

"You're talking Amber Alerts and nationwide attention if the father goes public. The FBI would be called in if we transport them across state lines."

"I'm betting he won't."

41

"And if you're wrong?"

Jill was caving. She could feel it. "Fire me. I'll take all the heat. The authorities won't even know ALIAS had anything to do with it. After all, I met Hannah at the shelter."

"I can't afford to fire you. I need you. My pool of qualified employees keeps shrinking." Jillian sat in the fancy formal chair, her head back and a weary expression on her face. "I'm not promising anything but let me look into the situation."

Kita knew she had her. "I'll get you the sister's hospital records."

"Okay," Jill said. "I'll consider temporary housing, in the District of Columbia. We can't move her or the kids across a state line and it can only be temporary until…unless we can prove the brother-in-law is dangerous."

Inside Kita was doing a serious fist pump. *Yes!* As long as she kept the judge happy and off Jillian's back, Hannah and her nieces would be safe.

"You won't regret this."

Jillian lifted her head. "I already do. But I don't have a choice."

Kita's smile was hurting her face. "Thank you. Thank you."

"It's going to take a few days to set up."

Kita didn't care. All she cared about was that Hannah and those girls had a chance now.

Jillian glanced at the slim Cartier tank on her wrist. "Come on. We've only got one hundred and five minutes to turn you into the judge's slut du jour."

"Slut?"

"Sorry, classy assistant aka new toy."

"Can't we blackmail the judge with that?"

"It's an open secret that he screws his office staff," Jillian said with disgust. "And they keep getting younger and younger. Horny old goat."

"You don't expect me to...."

"Of course not. But you may have to dodge him. The good news is Alex Saunders is a by-the-book agent. You won't ever be alone with the judge in a private setting."

"You know him?" Kita tried to act casual.

"I did a little checking while you were interviewing your suspect."

"Anything I should know?" She tried to keep the question casual but Jillian saw right through her.

"He's got a solid rep for following the rules." Jillian said with a sly smile, "You're interested."

Kita flushed. Maybe. But she only shrugged.

"He looked like he'd like to get to know you a whole lot better."

Kita blushed at Jill's teasing.

"He's going to have a cow when he figures out that Marsh and I worked for the Marshals and the reasons we left." Jillian's smile was not nice. "Make sure you don't spill any secrets if he screws you blind."

"Jill!" She could feel the embarrassment flood her face.

No chance of that happening.

Not if he followed the rules like Jillian thought he did.

"There's nothing that states that the protectorate can't get involved with someone from a different agency."

Okay the mind-reading was getting a little freaky. Better switch subjects to something a little more practical.

Office assistant and girlfriend, but bodyguard on the down low, for Judge Adams. Kita spent her days in yoga pants and workout tops. Her closet was full of Lucy and Title IX. Hardly the proper attire for this gig.

"I don't have the clothes for this assignment."

"Don't worry." Jillian went over to the desk and hit the intercom button. "Maria. Check out the closet in the spare bedroom. We need to outfit Kita for the judge, so bring the slinky stuff."

Oh boy.

Chapter 6

A lex sat in the antechamber of the judge's office and skimmed information on his phone.

The security just to get in the building was tight, and technically Alex shouldn't be in chambers when a confidential pretrial meeting was happening.

So he'd spent the past hour waiting out here and researching Adams-Larsen, the supposedly high-end public relations and consulting firm run by Jillian Larsen and Marsh Adams.

Except he hadn't been able to acquire much information. The general consensus was their client list was so exclusive and their work so confidential that no one knew who actually used their services. The research he'd garnered did nothing to reassure him that having one of their employees act as his backup was a good idea.

Alex was hamstrung between his personal code of conduct and the unusual circumstances of this protection detail.

Which meant the probability of a cluster-fuck was astronomical.

He hated that he'd barely started and the rules were being thrown out the window. The only way to maintain control of a situation was to follow the rules, especially with so many variables in play. He had to manage this operation. He had to supervise the unexpected operative. He had to control Judge Adams.

Alex's only hope was that when Kita Kim arrived, the judge would deem her completely unsuitable. Alex wasn't sure what would happen then but at least he'd have another chance to convince the judge to stick with an all Marshal protection detail.

Jesus, he didn't want her on this op. She was a distraction with her sensuality, quick wit, and smart mouth —he was crazy attracted to her even if she was all wrong for him.

She'd freaking executed a search on a suspect's computer without authorization. But more than her flaunting of proper procedure, which maybe he could forgive since she wasn't actually engaged in law enforcement activities, she was a danger to his peace of mind.

Perfect example. Right now he should be reviewing the emails sent to the judge, instead he was remembering her delicate scent and her strong fingers and the way she'd taken care of those plants for Mr. Gauss.

The dichotomy between tough girl and gentle soul intrigued him.

He didn't have time to be intrigued. He needed to get this case solved and hopefully get reinstated to his former position.

"Come in, Ms. Kim." Alex heard the disembodied voice of Judge Adams's receptionist. "Follow the hallway. The judge is in chambers but Mr. Saunders is expecting you."

The click of high heels on the gleaming wood floors

preceded Kita Kim's entrance. Alex found himself holding his breath.

She'd incited a carnal response from his body while she'd been sweaty and disheveled.

He didn't even want to speculate about his reaction to her when she was all spiffed up to be Judge Adams's staff aide slash playmate.

Kita Kim strode around the corner and into the antechamber with a determined purpose. Like a punch to the gut, her appearance sucked the breath out of his lungs and left him gasping for air.

His gaze locked onto her like a tractor beam pulling two separate forces together.

A few hours ago he'd been dropped off by a plain Asian woman with clear skin, slicked-back hair in a messy ponytail, and sculpted biceps in a tight spandex top. He was equal parts hopeful the judge wouldn't use her and scornful that the judge couldn't see her worth. Through it all he'd wondered how she would fare against the judge's obvious chauvinism. If Alex had the judge pegged, he liked them young, elegant, and sexily vacant.

Of which, the only one that applied to Kita was young. And even then he put her age at around twenty-eight or twenty-nine, so not too young.

She had transformed from the sweaty kick-ass girl to the businesslike employee, and now to a chic, sophisticated woman.

Wow. The exclamation slipped into his consciousness before he could censor it.

He was unable to stop staring, rooted to the floor by some indescribable force field. Her skin was flawless, a warm golden hue with the slightest blush of peach shimmering on her high cheekbones. Smoky charcoal shadowed the lids of her tilted eyes, and a liner emphasized the lush sweep of her thick black eyelashes.

Her mouth, Jesus, her mouth. The lush curve of her lower lip, slicked with a deep coral gloss, exuded the forbidden, and would tempt the pope to forsake his vows. The sharply defined muscles so clearly displayed by her workout shorts and tank top were expertly showcased by the form-fitting jade-green dress. The deep V of her neckline revealed her cleavage and her perfect handful-sized breasts. Her skin gleamed in the unforgiving office fluorescent light. The material hugged her curvy ass, ending just above the knee and revealing sleekly muscled legs. The final touches were the shiny pumps that matched the color of her lips and single smooth bracelet of pale celadon jade that circled her right wrist.

His brain supplied images of him slowly unzipping the classic tank dress and peeling away the clingy material to expose the plump curves of her breasts. He had a curious urge to run his tongue along the sharp curve of her collarbone.

Attraction sizzled through him, lighting up his veins and churning through his body. She made his blood run hot and his mind turn to exploits better left unimagined.

Kita Kim didn't back down, didn't look away, and yet he could still sense how absolutely uncomfortable she was with his scrutiny. She was hot and gorgeous and the judge was going to have his hands all over her. He couldn't explain why that thought zapped him with a lightning bolt of rage.

"Are you sure this is wise?" Alex stepped closer to her, his words soft, meant only for her. As if they existed inside their own private bubble, already connected on some tenth string of awareness. He had the disconcerting feeling that he could say anything to her no matter how shocking and she would take it in stride. Understanding him, understanding his lust-filled thoughts, as well as forgiving him with the same compassion she'd shown toward Mr. Gauss.

Why he thought she'd forgive him was beyond him and stupid, stupid, stupid.

"It's my job." She dismissed his concerns with a flicker of her eyelashes.

"I know you can hold your own physically." Alex complimented her but she just shrugged.

He ran his gaze over her trim form, hyperaware of the warm citrus scent wafting around her. Sweat sheened on her skin as he leaned imperceptibly closer. She shivered, a little shimmy of arousal. If he had run his hands over her bare skin, she couldn't have had a more immediate physical and sensual reaction to him. And dammit, he wanted to touch her. To drown in her. But that was a terrible idea. "You're quick, responsive, and intuitive."

"And that's a problem?" She quivered, and he could literally feel her desire to get away from him.

"No, but you're also a distraction." Alex took a step back. He skimmed his gaze over her. "I can't do my job if I'm more worried about the judge's reaction to you and protecting you from him than about him."

"Your feelings are your problem," she replied coolly. "I am not responsible for them."

Alex went cold at her words.

She'd used terminology frequently employed by victims, especially when coming to grips with being manipulated.

He pressed his lips together to stop from demanding to know who'd hurt her. He felt like a caveman and he was sure if he had a club he'd be beating it against his chest and howling at the moon.

"You're absolutely right." He didn't care if she was

right. He'd kick the ass of anyone who hurt her. Except she'd probably kick their ass all on her own. And damned if that didn't turn him on too.

Jesus, he was like one big walking hormone.

Resolutely he got his head back under control.

Kita said, "Have you got the letters? I'd like to take a look at them, then send copies to Jillian."

The rest of the intel Alex had learned in the past two hours came rushing back.

Jillian Larsen was a former US Marshal. She'd been suspended for sleeping with a witness, putting the trial and the witness's life in jeopardy. She'd been a disgrace to the Marshals and herself. If she hadn't resigned there was a good chance a full-on investigation might have been launched. But according to the gossip he'd uncovered, the powers that be hadn't wanted the negative publicity to blow up in the media. So they'd let her walk.

Alex's lip curled. Jillian Larsen was the worst kind of agent. The kind who thought the rules didn't apply to her, thought she was above the regulations, and jeopardized everyone in her path without a care for the consequences.

When she'd left the agency, she'd taken Marshall Adams with her and they'd started a PR agency. In a Venn diagram of PR and US Marshals, the intertwined circles would have very little overlap. What the hell PR had to do with their former business Alex had no idea. And he didn't understand why the judge wanted Adams-Larsen to be involved in his protection.

He was shocked his boss was okay with giving Larsen's agency access to the judge's case. Keep the judge happy. That was his first and foremost directive, after keeping him safe, of course.

Kita propped her fists on her hips, bringing his attention

back to her. She obviously knew her boss's background and didn't care.

He needed to get over the zing of attraction. He had to be extra diligent. He couldn't afford to have Kita Kim fuck up the judge's protection. And since he now knew what kind of agency she worked for—image consulting, ha—he had to be extra careful, guarding the judge from the threat of harm but also from the potential risk of incompetency.

Just because he wanted to throw her down on a bed and spend hours exploring her body didn't mean he would. And just because the attraction was mutual didn't mean it was going anywhere. Not if he had anything to say about it.

"Are you going to share copies of the threats?"

"It's not necessary." His need to hold on to that intelligence was a little over the top. "We've got the OPI, Office of Professional Intelligence, analyzing and dissecting the threats against Judge Adams. It's possible that some of the information is classified."

"Then give me redacted versions," she demanded impatiently. "I want to put together some idea of what kind of crazy we're up against."

He repeated his earlier statement. "The Marshals have a team working on it."

Kita cocked her hip and held out her hand. Her mouth, glossed with the color of a ripe peach, compressed into a flat line. "Not. Negotiable."

Alex considered her for a moment. He could continue to refuse. The judge's protection was considered a highly sensitive detail.

As he looked at the flat expression in her vivid black eyes he didn't guess she'd have anything to add but as long as she didn't let anyone else see them…. "You can read them in the car on the way to the judge's residence."

"I'm bringing my own car."

"Not negotiable." He threw the words back at her. "You are now under the rules and regulations of the US Marshal's office regarding witness and high-value target protection."

"Explain."

"You're with me." Alex wasn't crazy about this next part, but he had no choice. The judge wanted extra protection, the Marshals weren't about to let anyone else mess up his security detail. "Permanently."

"You mean—"

"I go everywhere the judge goes during the day." Alex may have gotten this detail because he'd been too vocal in his disapproval of his last witness. As a result, he had a notation in his personnel file. He wasn't about to get another. That meant he wasn't about to break any rules, so she'd just have to suck it up. "And so do you."

"So…."

"We're stuck with each other."

Chapter 7

Fuck a duck.

Kita thought she'd have a little more time to get used to being around Alex Saunders. His disapproval of her methods stung. So her inconvenient attraction was even more mystifying. Or maybe she could figure out the perpetrator after reviewing the letters, and never have to see this guy again. He certainly ran hot and cold. And her reaction to him was even more puzzling.

She might be out of practice but she knew when a guy was interested. And he'd been hotter than DC in July until suddenly a switch flipped and he'd looked at her like something stuck to the bottom of his shoe.

Whatever.

Now she had to spend every moment with him? Maybe he had a partner and they could switch.

Alex Saunders twisted his arm to glance at the watch strapped to his thick raw-boned wrist. Kita swallowed as she realized she'd been right. He was much bigger than he appeared.

She'd always had a thing for big guys.

"The judge should be done momentarily."

She blinked, reined in her wayward thoughts. She still had to pass the judge's approval. Which she *had* to do. Hannah Smith was depending on her. "Okay."

"I'll bring the car around." Alex shifted his attention to Kita. "You have a weapon?"

"Of course."

"And you're certified to carry?"

He was starting to really piss her off. "Of course."

Everyone at ALIAS was certified and they had to go through re-certification every three months to keep that status. Everyone on their staff was multitalented and proficient in more than one area of expertise.

"Okay. You escort the judge to the garage exit and I'll pick you up there. We can stop at your car and get your bag. We're headed to the judge's co-op in the Watergate so he can dress for the fundraiser dinner."

His autocratic tone set her nerves on edge. Kita held her tongue but it was difficult. "Yes, sir." She fought the urge to salute.

He nodded abruptly. "Once we get to the judge's house we can go over protocol for the evening."

Before she could reply, the judge burst from behind the tall mahogany doors, followed by a petite redhead in a tailored navy suit. He stopped dead. The woman almost ran into the back of him before she jerked to his side and caught herself on the tips of her too-high stilettos.

The judge stared.

Kita flushed.

"It appears that I was incorrect." His smile made her want to take a super-hot shower. Yuck. "You'll do just fine."

Double yuck.

The petite redhead with the perfect makeup and nails

that could rip Kita's skin to shreds glared at her as if Kita were some sort of stain on her low-cut pristine white blouse.

The judge studied her for another long minute. His still black eyebrows lowered over eyes the same shape as her pal Marsh, but that was the only similarity she'd noticed. He narrowed his gaze. "You look familiar. Have we met before?"

Kita's pulse danced the rhumba in her throat. She'd lived next door to Marsh and his mother for years. It was possible that the judge had met her mother on one of his infrequent visits to see his son. But not Kita.

"No, sir."

"Call me Bobby." The judge swung his arm around her shoulders, his palm dropping dangerously low to her breast. Kita gritted her teeth and dredged up a smile. Everything in her wanted to shove his hand away and shrug off the casual embrace.

One good stomp to his instep would likely accomplish both. And quickly.

But if she blew this assignment, she would let Hannah down. And she couldn't do that. So she'd suck it up, and do whatever it took to make the judge happy.

Mr. Stick Up His Butt was right. They were stuck with each other. Kita hadn't backed down from a fight since she was seventeen and she wasn't about to start now. This time the stakes were high and she would not fail.

She would do everything in her power to make sure Hannah and those kids were safe.

She made a show of checking her weapon, casually throwing off the judge's hand before it could start to wander.

"Vanessa, I'm done for the day."

"You've got Congresswoman Nichols's fundraiser

tonight." Something in the woman's voice caused Kita to take another look at the assistant. But Vanessa's face had settled into a bland, professional mask. "Do you need a car for your plus one?"

"It's in my phone calendar, dear." The judge didn't even look at his assistant as he smiled at Kita. "And my date is right here."

Vanessa nodded sharply, shot daggers at Kita. "Have a good time." But somehow Kita thought she was really saying *choke on your chicken dinner*.

"Judge, I'd like to ask you some questions about the letters when we get you back to your house."

"Don't trouble yourself with that." He literally patted her on the head.

"It's no trouble." She smiled tightly. "After all, it is my job."

He sighed. "Then I'll have Vanessa shoot you copies."

After rattling off her email address, the ever-efficient but slightly hostile Vanessa forwarded the emails right away.

Kita analyzed the text on the way to the judge's co-op.

The wording was sometimes a tad strange, as if potentially the sender spoke more than one language. A misplaced article or adjective. Nothing in the syntax jumped out to indicate a specific derivative. Although based on the judge's nonchalant attitude toward the threats, she began to suspect there was more going on than he copped to.

Kita needed access to his email server to trace the menacing emails. Because they were online, the danger to the judge should seem less worrisome. Internet threats could be delivered from anywhere in the world, and the perpetrator could in actuality not have any close access to the judge.

You will pay for your crimes. I will not be ignored. I want to carve out your heart. While there was some gruesome wording, when she asked why he was being guarded twenty-four seven, the judge put his hand on her knee, precipitating a very strained and awkward conversation about why touching her was off-limits.

That was fun.

And yet he'd managed to distract her enough that the answer was lost. But she would get back to it.

After they arrived at his co-op, the judge went to change into formal attire, leaving her alone with Alex.

Judge Adams's co-op was on one of the top floors of the Watergate complex. Kita bet the mortgage on his five-thousand-square-foot condo was insane.

However the building did have decent security.

Kita had suited up for the upcoming charity event. She had a knife strapped to her inner thigh, and a small caliber handgun in her sequined purse. Odds were she wouldn't need either.

Alex handed her a small comm piece. She tried to tuck it in the shell of her ear but a strand of her hair got caught in between her ear and the device.

"Let me." Alex's husky rasp whispered over her ear as he bent to ease the strand from where it had gotten pinned. His warm breath brushed along her bare neck, and up close his tightly leashed power surrounded her.

His broad shoulders seemed to expand as he inhaled deeply. "Got it."

She wanted to get something. Kita tilted her chin up so she could look him in the eye. But he was closer than she realized. So close she could see the flecks of navy and the darker ring surrounding his silvery blue eyes. The heat that he'd kept banked earlier flared to life again.

The air around them shimmered with anticipation.

Everything in her quickened, stirred, *wanted*. Her body seemed to instinctively ready for his touch; her lips buzzed with anticipation as his gaze dropped to her mouth. She'd eaten off all the lipstick earlier with her frustration when the judge had dodged her questions.

Alex's hand rested on the curve where her neck met her shoulder. His palm was hot against the beat of her pulse and he stroked his fingertips along her bare collarbones. She didn't think he was aware he was touching her but she was hyperconscious of every single fingertip and the rough callused skim of his fingers against her sensitive skin.

Her breasts swelled and her sex softened, trembling on the edge of desire as she yearned for him to bend closer and press his lips to hers.

She swayed toward him, and her breasts brushed his hard pecs. The diamond points of her nipples were ultra-sensitized through the layers of fabric that separated their chests.

God, he was so close. His breath soughed against her lips.

Her mouth dried, and she swiped her tongue over her lips for moisture in the suddenly arid room. Anticipation was like a lick of heat rising to consume them in a mutual fire.

Alex tilted his head and her eyes drifted closed.

His lips, soft, yet not, brushed hers. The contact was light, insignificant, and yet the moment was fraught with sexual tension. They hovered on the edge, one slight move could tip them together or apart. Kita couldn't stand it. She nipped his bottom lip.

The tension broke and they surged against each other, the attraction mutual and intense. His palms surrounded her ribcage, and she lifted her hands and gripped his forearms, holding tight to the leashed power in his hard muscles. Her body tingled with arousal.

He held her tightly, keeping them a short distance apart. The press of his mouth was more forceful this time but still exploratory. With each brush of his lips he advanced, pressing a kiss to the corners of her mouth, then swirled his tongue over her lips.

Kita's mouth parted, letting him in. She met the next sweep of his tongue with hers, the intimate contact like an electrical zap.

He pushed his tongue inside as hers tangled with his. Their lips fused, as he dove into the kiss. Eager, skilled, he played her mouth like a virtuoso. Unwilling to break for air, they dueled for supremacy.

His muscles were rock hard beneath her hands. She wanted to twine around him and get as close as possible but even through the intense, powerful kiss, he held her slightly away from him. Not letting their bodies touch.

Until his erection brushed against her belly.

Kita moaned. Softly, deeply.

The mechanical click of a lock, and the sound of a door being opened, shot through her brain. They jumped apart. Alex had his weapon out. Kita reached for her knife, chest heaving, heart thundering. Until the judge's slow, deliberate footsteps sounded from the hallway that led to the bedrooms.

She straightened, pressed the flat of her palm against her lips in a deliberate move, as if she could wipe away the erotic, mesmerizing minutes.

Alex quickly holstered his weapon. His hooded gaze hid whatever he was feeling but he turned away from her quickly. He pretended an excessive interest in the sweeping view of the Potomac river, dismissing her without a flicker of acknowledgement that the kiss even happened.

Kita lifted her chin. *Fuck him.*

She retrieved her gloss from her purse and hastily applied a new layer of coral stain to her lips.

The judge strode into the room just as she dropped the tube into her small clutch. His shiny tuxedo shoes halted, and he squinted at the two of them standing twenty feet apart. Kita knew her lips were likely puffy, but that couldn't be helped.

The judge assessed Alex, then Kita. His eyes narrowed. "Let's go."

They hadn't fooled him at all. And he was not happy.

Chapter 8

O n the judge's arm, Kita roamed the Top of the Hay
banquet room, at the exclusive downtown DC Hotel.
The L-shaped room only held about three hundred and
fifty people, not including the servers. The French doors
were open to the terrace, and the illuminated White House
glowed in the backdrop of the early fall sunset.

Alex had chosen chauffeur duty, sticking with the judge's
limo so that no one could tamper with it. The threats were
vague enough that a car bomb had to remain on the list as a
potential way to off the guy. *You won't see me coming.* Had so
many connotations and possibilities.

Although it did give them a clue. Whether it was valid or
not. Won't see *me* coming indicated a single perpetrator. So
they needed to concentrate on an individual rather than a
group who might be upset with Judge Adams or one of his
rulings.

Kita wondered if Alex had picked limo duty so he
wouldn't have to work close to her. A momentary stab of
hurt surprised her. Then pissed her off. She didn't care if

Alex freaking Saunders didn't want to spend time in her company.

His partner, Sheppard Gaffney, was at the fundraiser somewhere. Kita had yet to meet him in person, but they were connected through their comm pieces.

"Remember, your job is to scan for anyone out of the ordinary or with an unhealthy interest in the judge. Point them out and Shep will handle the physical protection aspect."

Kita resisted the urge to roll her eyes. He'd quoted the Marshal's manual no less than five times while they'd gone over the plan for tonight. She seriously wondered if he slept with the damn thing.

And there was a place she shouldn't go. Alex in bed. His black hair tousled and day-old stubble roughening his cheeks and highlighting his mouth. That perpetual guardedness stripped away.

But more than that, an insidious attraction slithered through her like a snake through the garden. She didn't like it. For the most part, men left her cold. Sure, she had male friends, but with the exception of Marsh, she was never quite at ease around them. She knew it was because of her background, but she didn't really care. Most men tended to let you down. Actually most *people* tended to let you down.

Vulnerability gave people the impression that you were a potential victim.

She would never be a victim again.

Her face frozen into the fakest of smiles, she kept her gaze moving and her body language all about appearing to be totally into the judge.

She'd finally understood that Judge Adams didn't really want a bodyguard. That was why he'd insisted on a woman.

Which was how she ended up playing arm candy to the randy old man.

Everyone she'd been introduced to thought she was his mistress.

She'd met three judges, four Congressmen—two of whom discreetly indicated that when she was done with the judge they'd have an opening—and several aides who all politely sneered at her when introduced. Clearly the judge's reputation preceded him.

So far she'd had to remove his hand from her ass three times.

Every time, she reminded herself that Hannah and those kids were counting on her. That she could handle a little inconvenient harassment if it meant getting Hannah and the kids away from a violent abusive man.

But when his palm started straying again, Kita pretended to whisper in the judge's ear. "Judge." She smiled and narrowed her gaze.

His deep-set eyes lit with an avaricious glee. "Yes, my dear."

"If you touch my butt one more time, I'll break your fingers," she murmured, too softly for anyone but the judge's ears.

And shit, she should not have said that. Hannah was depending on her.

Hell, even Jill was depending on her.

"Seriously?" Alex growled low in his throat, the sound completely audible through her ear piece. Fortunately, the judge was not dialed in to their security channel.

The judge slid his hand back to the curve of her waist.

She patted his fingers to let him know that was better.

That kind of attention she could handle. It was

predictable. But Alex's gruff voice in her ear, swearing quietly, loosened some of the tension in her body.

The congresswoman of the hour, Darla Nichols, strode up to them, an interested gleam in her eye. There was an easy familiarity in the way she stood so closely to Judge Adams, as if they knew each other on a more intimate level.

"Darla, lovely to see you again." The esteemed congresswoman from Pennsylvania was the reason they were attending this fundraiser. Her five-grand-a-ticket cocktail party was to raise money for her upcoming tough reelection campaign. Her opponent had deep pockets and a wealthy benefactor.

"Thank you for supporting my campaign, Judge," Darla said smoothly. Her gaze skimmed over Kita and dismissed her with a blink. Perfect. She preferred to fade into the background.

"Darla took over her husband's seat when he died of a heart attack about a month into his second term," Judge Adams said. "I am a huge admirer. As you well know."

The judge was clearly connected.

The congresswoman smiled again and whispered conspiratorially, "Got to keep on your good side after the Secretary of Labor scandal."

The judge held one of her hands between his palms.

"I'd love it if you'd put in a good word for me after I win," she said softly.

The judge raised a brow. "Which committee?"

Kita tuned out the conversation. She didn't really care which committee the congresswoman hoped to get on. Her job was to search the crowd for any possible threats.

A waiter approached their group with a single scotch on a platter. "For you, sir."

Kita frowned. There were plenty of bars set up around

the perimeter of the room. The black pants and white-shirt-clad waitstaff were only passing hors d'oeuvres.

And as far as she could see, no one else was getting a drink from a waiter.

"Champagne, please," she demanded to the waiter. Who blinked in surprise.

As the judge reached out to take the highball glass, Kita "accidentally" tripped. But the waiter seemed to see her coming and shifted forward. The judge's hand closed around the glass and Kita had no choice but to bring her arm down on the judge's wrist. She put an extra oomph in the move and he lost his grip. The glass shattered on the wooden parquet flooring, sending glass shards and liquid splattering against her bare legs, the congresswoman's long black dress, and Judge Adams's shiny shoes.

The waiter had jumped back.

The crowd noise disguised most of the sound of the glass breaking apart so only the people nearest them turned around.

"What the hell?" The judge didn't raise his voice but his displeasure was very apparent.

"I'm so sorry, sir," Kita placed her hand on the judge's tuxedo jacket right over his heart. Pretending remorse, she leaned in and said clearly, "We need to get out of here."

"I don't want to leave," the judge said crabbily.

"Code red?" Alex asked, the concern in his voice came through loud and clear.

"I need to leave, Judge Adams." Kita's legs were tingling, and she didn't think it had a damn thing to do with the cuts from the broken glass. "I'm feeling a tad faint."

Under-fucking statement of the year.

"Shit," Alex breathed in her ear. "Shep."

"On it." She recognized Shep's voice from their sound

check. "Coming in hot. I'm the blond dude in a black tux. I'll be there momentarily."

"You shouldn't have been so clumsy." The judge's haughty reprimand set her on edge. But they had bigger problems.

Kita squeezed his arm. Hard. "We need to leave, Bobby."

"I can have my driver drop you at home…later, if you want to stay, Judge." The congresswoman's smile confirmed that she and the judge had been more intimately acquainted in the past.

"Judge Adams. Nice to see you again." Shep came straight toward Kita and then circled around so he was on her right. "Your date doesn't look so good. We should probably get her to the sick room."

The judge was going to argue.

"Please, sir."

"I'll have to take a raincheck, Darla." The judge bussed the woman's cheek and gallantly took Kita's arm.

Kita didn't have to pretend to be faint. The tingling had turned into an all-out fire on her skin. As soon as they moved away from the congresswoman, Kita said, "You need to get the judge out of here."

Her breath had begun to drag in her chest, each inhale a workout as her lungs constricted as if she was being squeezed in a bear hug.

"Shep, you aren't leaving her there," Alex said sharply.

"Of course not. What's wrong with you?" Shep demanded quietly.

"I don't know. Poison, maybe?" Kita gasped rawly. "You need to find out where the waiter got that glass."

They hustled to the express elevator and within a few minutes they escorted the judge out the front door, where the limo was idling. The judge helped Kita in and then Shep practically shoved the judge in after her.

Alex peeled away discreetly, not so fast as to call attention to their departure, but with purpose.

"Shit." Alex swore from the driver's seat. "We've got to get her to a medic."

The judge sat across from Kita, studying her intently. "You think that was meant for me?" His face had whitened.

She bobbed her head, trying to control her muscles.

"Any ideas what it was?" Alex took a corner with too much speed.

"Fast-acting." Kita tried to think calmly. She hadn't even ingested it. Some of the liquid had merely splashed on her legs and possibly entered her bloodstream through the cuts from the broken glass.

"What other symptoms?"

"Elevated heart rate, constricted airways, sweating." She tried to get her mouth to move, but forming the words felt like trying to talk under water. Slurred speech, disoriented, slow processing of details, she forced herself to focus on the precisely trimmed hair on the back of Alex's head. She listed off her symptoms as if they weren't happening to her. Meanwhile, sweat coated her skin and her heart threatened to pound right out of her chest.

"Anaphylactic?" Alex was trying to make his voice calm —how she knew that was a mystery, but she knew.

"Maybe?" But rational thought filtered through her panicking brain. "Might be an allergic reaction."

"What are you allergic to?"

"Aspirin." Kita's vision shorted—white dots swam in her eyes, blurring her focus, and the world slowly faded to opaque. "Don't worry about me. I'm a survivor."

ALEX JERKED to a stop at the hospital emergency room entrance. As soon as Kita mentioned the poison possibility, he'd called in a doctor the marshals worked with to meet them at this facility. But he had to get her inside. Pronto.

"Stay. R-ith sh-udge," Kita argued.

Bobby Adams had been remarkably quiet.

Shit. She was correct. Technically Alex should wait until someone could get her inside and he should stand guard over the judge. Especially since she was reacting to some substance meant for their protectee.

"Not leaving you here." Alex shut off the engine and rounded the side of the car. He yanked open the limo door. Her face was so pale, her lips nearly white. Sweat coated her skin and the hair at her temple was soaked.

He couldn't just leave her in the car for someone to eventually come get her, and he couldn't abandon the judge. The rules were extremely clear on that directive. The protectee's safety was first priority.

But fuck.

Kita had fallen unconscious. Her breathing was labored. He had to get her inside the hospital. Now.

But he also couldn't leave the judge alone.

Alex lifted Kita into his arms, another break in protocol. If anyone attacked the judge right now, Alex did not have his hands free. His thoughts, normally measured, precise and focused, bounced all over the place.

He'd have to take the judge with him.

"Let's go, Judge." Dammit, for her big personality, she was awfully light in his arms.

"I can just stay right—"

"She's going into shock because she stopped you from

ingesting a tainted drink," Alex snarled. "Get your ass out of the car."

The panic he was trying to suppress plowed to the surface of his consciousness. Fuck him.

Finally, the judge seemed to realize that his position was precarious.

"I'll have another team here momentarily to escort you home." Alex said, "But right now, I need you to come with me so that this young woman can get treatment and I can keep you protected." No time for polite niceties. "Get moving."

Alex barreled through the emergency room doors and bypassed the main waiting room crammed with people. Dr. Sharmila Patel had her own private practice inside the Beltway but she also had privileges at this hospital.

His feet thudded on the linoleum as he ran toward the outpatient surgery department, trying unsuccessfully not to jostle Kita. The bright fluorescent overhead light seared his eyes, the burn keeping him focused on getting her into the exam room, rather than the terror ripping apart his insides.

The judge didn't quite keep pace with him. But he wasn't far behind. Thank God.

Alex didn't know what he would do if the judge fell back farther. He wanted to concentrate on the woman in his arms, but his responsibilities pulled him in two directions, taut, like a rubber band stretched beyond its natural elasticity. He was at his limits between duty and need, and he didn't know if he would snap back, or break.

The surgery center was closed this time of night, but Dr. Patel met them at the doorway and gestured Alex inside. The door closed behind the judge with a quiet snick.

"How is she presenting?"

Alex listed off her symptoms. "We think she was poisoned but it could also be an allergic reaction."

He laid her down on the hospital bed, taking care to protect her head from banging on the cushioned table. The silky strands of her hair tangled in his fingers and he remembered their kiss. Remembered the longing he'd suppressed. He'd wanted to thread his fingers through that thick curtain and fist her hair in his hand and hold her captive while he plundered her.

Goddammit.

The doctor efficiently propped up Kita's feet, then began her exam.

"Did she ingest the poison?" Mila was running her nitrile-clad fingers over Kita.

Get your fucking head in this room, Saunders.

Kita's head lolled to the side, her breathing compromised, thick and wheezy in the shadowed examination room. The bank of equipment—oxygen machines, heart rate monitors, and EKG machines—behind the doctor stayed silent.

"I don't think so." Impotent with rage, he clenched his fists to stop from reaching out and stroking those sweaty strands away from her face. To stop himself from whispering in her ear that he wouldn't let anything or anyone hurt her.

He certainly hadn't done a stellar job up until this point.

"Glass broke, some of the liquid splashed on her legs." The judge spoke from the corner where he'd slumped. "There may be cuts."

The doctor examined her legs, small dried blood spots dotted her shins, but none of them looked deep. Even though Mila wasn't a crime scene tech, maybe they could get something from Kita's skin.

The doctor directed Alex. "Flip on the monitors over there."

She tilted Kita's head back and stuck her fingers in her throat, then lifted her eyelids. "Dilated pupils," she murmured, "constricted airway, difficulty breathing. She's got all the markers of anaphylactic shock but I won't know what she's been exposed to until I see some blood work."

Alex wasn't a doctor, but even he could tell Kita was struggling. "Do we have that long?"

"No." Her luminous black eyes and the crinkle between her eyebrows told the story. With crisp efficiency, she wrapped rubber tubing around Kita's biceps and thumped the vein in the crook of her arm. The blue vein popped quickly, and she deftly inserted a needle, withdrawing a vial of blood in seconds. She dabbed the insertion point with cotton and wrapped a Band-Aid over the cotton. "I'm going to have to give her a dose of adrenaline and then epinephrine."

"English, Sharmila."

"Like an epi-pen but more intense."

"Will it save her?"

"Probably." Mila bit her plump lip. "Unless it works with whatever else in her bloodstream and makes the effects worse."

She attached a blood pressure cuff to Kita's arm, slipped the oxygen mask over Kita's mouth and nose and continued to monitor her vitals. In the meantime, Kita's heart rate was slowing, and even through the oxygen mask her breathing was labored.

Fuck.

Judicial Security Division protocol dictated that he not leave his protectee unattended. Especially with the imminent threat to Judge Adams's safety. Right now Alex was so pissed at Judge Adams his brain was one wrong word from exploding in rage.

He needed to get the judge out of here. Alex quickly made a call to HQ requesting backup since he didn't know when his partner would be free. Right now, Shep was busy interrogating the waiter who'd delivered the drink at the fundraiser.

Mila was on the phone, likely consulting with another doctor.

Alex couldn't stand it any longer. He needed to touch her. To feel her life force. To let her know that he would protect her while she couldn't protect herself. He gripped her hand, pressing her palm between his like a prayer. Her soft skin was delicate and feminine beneath his rougher hands.

Acid pitched and rolled in his stomach, battering away at the lining as possible consequences scrolled through his mind at a dizzying speed. He breathed—in and out—in time with her, as if by sheer will he could force her to continue breathing. "Keep fighting," Alex whispered in her ear. "I won't let anything happen to you. But you've got to meet me halfway, Kita. Keep fighting. Dammit."

Mila put her cold palm over Alex and Kita's clasped hands. "I'm sorry, I'm going to have to give this to her. We just have to hope there isn't an adverse interaction between the adrenaline and whatever is in her system. We can't wait because her symptoms are getting worse."

Alex inhaled, holding the breath in his lungs. *Ba-bump* echoed in his ears along with a rushing noise as she injected Kita.

There was no change.

"Nothing is happening."

"Alex, take it down a notch." But the doctor was

sweating. "We have to wait fifteen minutes to see if the adrenaline works."

Alex held Kita's hand in a tight grip. She was so small and delicate.

He studied everything Mila was doing. She set up the IV pole and started a drip of fluid. "What's that?"

"Right now it's just fluid, but if the adrenaline takes and her symptoms start to subside, I'll add some antihistamines. If it doesn't, I'll give her some epinephrine next."

They waited in silence. Mila continued to fuss over Kita, then she adjusted the oxygen mask and rolled her onto her side.

"What are you doing now?"

"Putting her in the recovery position in case she vomits." Mila propped her fists on her hips. "Do I ask you what you're doing every time you go to work?"

Jesus. He was acting like a maniac.

But he couldn't bear that she had been hurt on his watch. And he'd broken protocol bringing Kita in. What if someone had gone after the judge while Alex was carrying her? After his brother was hurt when they were kids he'd learned to follow the rules, always. When you ignored policies, bad things happened. "Sorry, Mila."

Mila rolled off the nitrile gloves and squeezed his biceps. "I know."

His phone buzzed on his hip. But he didn't want to let go of Kita's hand.

He shifted so he could pull out his phone without releasing her from his grip. Alex answered one handed, never taking his gaze from the rise and fall of her chest. "Saunders."

"Where are you?" It was Shep. "I'm here."

"Come back to the outpatient operating suite."

He hung up. Alex watched Kita for any additional sign of distress.

"I'm going to take this to the lab myself and request the results stat." The doctor held up the vial of blood, shook the contents. "I'll be right back."

"Are you sure it's okay to leave?"

"It will be five minutes at the most." But then Mila hesitated. "Press this red button if her breathing starts to worsen or she throws up."

Alex listened the monitors intently, never taking his gaze from Kita, obsessively watching her chest rise and fall.

Right after Mila left, Shep arrived in the surgery suite. "Any intelligence?"

Shep stood across Kita's body and propped his hands on his hip. Alex shot a quick glance at him before shifting his attention back to Kita.

"Very little. A woman in a black dress gave him the drink and a twenty-dollar bill to give it to Judge Adams."

"A woman. In a black dress. At a political fundraiser." Disgust rumbled through him. That wouldn't be a problem.

"With big boobs." Shep's mouth twitched.

"A woman with breasts." Alex wanted to swear. Jesus Christ on a cracker.

"*Big* breasts." Shep clarified.

The judge piped up from his seat. "A woman?"

Yeah, that was interesting.

"We did get one other piece of info." Shep snapped back to seriousness and lost the smirk. "White woman."

"Which rules out maybe half or less of the attendees."

"You're assuming she had a ticket," the judge said.

That would also narrow their list of their potential suspects. The ticket price was sky-high. Jilted lover? Except that the judge tended to "date" much younger women who either worked for him or in some capacity at the courts. They wouldn't have the cash to buy a ticket. However, the mysterious woman might be the wife of someone he'd put away. Just like Mr. Gauss from this morning, another disgruntled spouse could be making the threats.

Alex said, "Let's get the list of ticket attendees and comb through it for any connections to the judge and his cases."

The glass was likely a nonstarter.

Shep confirmed Alex's thoughts. "The glass shattered into too many pieces to get any prints."

Alex clutched at any thought that might give them intelligence like he clutched Kita's hand. "What about the bill?"

Shep rolled his eyes. "Alex, you know how many fingerprints are on money."

"But you got it."

"Of course I got it, but it's probably a dead end."

Alex's brain clicked along. So far they had no actionable intelligence. "So we have to wait for the toxicology report to come back."

"Yeah."

Alex ran the fingers of his free hand through his hair. "A woman. Close up and personal. Not somewhere far away and online. She was in that damn room. Can we get security tapes?"

"Already on it," Shep said.

"Obviously not on it enough since Kita is lying here unconscious." Alex swallowed, afraid his voice was going to break. What the hell was wrong with him? He didn't even want Adams-Larsen or Kita Kim on this case.

Shep raised his brows.

And okay, yeah, he was slightly out of control.

Mila took that moment to come back into the room. Shep had his weapon out and pointed at her within seconds.

She yelped and jumped back. Her thick-lashed eyes widened. "What in the hell are you doing? You don't bring a weapon into a house of healing."

Alex said drily, "Deputy Marshal Sheppard Gaffney meet Dr. Sharmila Patel."

Shep paused, gathered his control back, then tucked his weapon into the leather holster at his waist. He mustered a lazy grin and held out his hand. "Call me Shep."

"Pass." She dismissed him and bent over Kita.

Blink. Blink. Alex didn't think he'd ever seen his pal Shep at a loss for words. He was one of those guys who was slick and yet likable. People, women especially, warmed to him right away.

Shep audibly snapped shut his jaw.

And if Alex wasn't one second away from losing his shit, he would have laughed. "Shouldn't she be awake by now?"

"It's not an exact science. But…."

His heart jumped in his throat. "What?"

Jesus, what if she was getting worse?

"Alex, she's responding positively."

He looked closer at Kita. Her skin color had warmed, a faint blush of peach covered her cheeks. Her lips were still deathly pale but the room was much quieter. Her breathing had softened, steadied, no longer struggling to escape her traumatized body.

The judge shuffled over to the gurney where Kita rested. "She really is going to be okay?" His brash front had subdued as if he finally realized the gravity of Kita's condition.

"I still need the tox screens back, and her vitals should be monitored for the next twenty-four hours but—" Mila checked the machines, ran her palms down Kita's arms, and lifted her hand to inspect her fingernails "—right now her prognosis appears good."

"Thank goodness." The judge slumped. "I really didn't think…."

"No, you didn't." Now that Kita was going to be okay, Alex was going to let Judge Adams have it. "The second she told you it was time to leave you should have listened."

"Uh, Alex."

"What the *hell* were you thinking?" Alex let go of Kita's hand and began to pace. His shoulders bunched around his ears and his hands clenched into fists. "You put Ms. Kim and yourself in danger."

"I didn't actually think the threat was real."

Alex fumed. "Then why the hell did you want Adams-Larsen on the case?"

"Uh, Alex." Shep's tone finally got through to him.

"Yeah?" he snarled.

"Can I talk to you? Outside?" Shep smiled at the doctor, pouring on his considerable charm. His non-gun hand gripped Alex's arm, hard. "We'll be right back."

Once the door to the surgery suite closed behind them, Alex yanked his arm from his grasp. "What do you want?"

He couldn't stand being away from Kita. The barrier of the shut door had him jonesing to confirm she was okay, still breathing. His heart rate accelerated like he was the one who'd just been injected with a syringe full of adrenaline. Shep grabbed his head and forced him to look at him. "Alex, what is happening here?"

"What?" But he was only half paying attention.

"You were yelling at your security protectee."

"I'd hardly call that yelling." Alex shook his head. "And the judge was totally out of line."

"Mr. By-The-Book Saunders isn't thinking clearly, or acting properly."

Shep's words stopped him cold. He was right. Alex was acting totally out of character. Like she'd cast some sorcery over him and he'd let things like duty, and protocol, and regulations just slip away from him without taking a deliberate step toward anarchy.

Hadn't he just been thinking about how important it was to follow protocol?

Alex dropped his head to stare at the shiny linoleum flooring. The ripples in the bluish gray and black pattern swam before his eyes as he unfocused and reviewed the past hour. He had acted emotionally, without thinking through the consequences. That could have had major repercussions on the judge, himself, the US Marshals. What the hell had he been thinking?

He needed to rein in his emotions and get back to the rules. Get back to the way he'd done things in the past. "Okay. Yes." He gritted out one last word: "Sorry."

"Everything's fine. It's just…not like you." Shep slapped a meaty hand on his shoulder.

"I'm good now." Or at least he would be. He needed to pull it together. It was his responsibility to protect the judge. His responsibility to make sure that no one got to his protectee. And he'd failed.

His mouth dry and his palms sweaty, Alex contemplated what he'd almost done. No more distractions.

He had to keep his eye on his goal to protect the judge.

Chapter 9

Kita woke up in a strange room.

The bed was cushy, the walls light gray, and the furniture what she considered Old World pompous. Her apartment was a riot of color and an eclectic mix of Asian and American, kinda like her.

Her head thumped, a rhythmic throbbing pulsing behind her left eye. She jammed her hands against her temples, trying to relieve the pressure and desperately attempting to remember what the hell happened.

Her scrambled brain reached for memories, for details, for anything. Was she hungover? She couldn't remember the last time she'd been drunk. Alcohol and her heritage didn't mix well. Although, if anything could drive her there it was likely Mr. Tall, Dark, and Pain in the Ass Saunders.

She had the oddest recollection of him hovering over her, whispering in her ear. The memory lingered just out of reach, like a veil draped over her mind, obscuring things.

She rolled to her back and nearly let out a scream.

Alex Saunders was in the bed next to her. He lay on top of the comforter. His blue-black hair stood straight up in unruly spikes, and day-old stubble dusted his jaw and upper lip. Like her earlier fantasy come to life, he'd lost the manual up his butt. This rumpled, scruffy, fresh-from-bed guy was far too appealing.

Even though her head was pounding, her body perked up and took notice.

Hot guy alert.

Sunlight streamed in between the curtains. He turned his head to look at her, casting his face in shadows. "You're awake." He stared as if trying to see inside her to where all her secrets and fears lurked. His gazed trailed over her face and shoulders.

Kita drew the covers up, just now realizing she wore only a lacy bra and panties beneath the cool sheets.

"What are you doing here?" she croaked. Her chapped lips split as she tried to swallow away her confusion.

"You needed to be monitored for twenty-four hours." Alex sat up. He was still dressed but he'd exchanged his suit pants for jeans and his jacket and tie were MIA. The blue button-down with rolled-up sleeves emphasized his corded forearms as he rubbed his callused fingers over his face.

"So *you* stayed with me?"

That seemed out of character for the uptight by-the-book agent who'd tried to shoot her down yesterday.

His fair skin flushed. "Doc said you needed someone to stay with you," he repeated stubbornly.

Oookay. Huh. But as the implications sank in, she acknowledged that she owed him. "Thank you then." She couldn't help it, the thanks was grudging.

The bed depressed next to her as he leaned closer, studying her. Looking for weakness?

His eyebrows arched down. Alex Saunders reached out,

his fingertips brushed her hair away from her face. Her skin buzzed where his fingers touched. "How are you feeling?"

She girded her thoughts and cleared her throat. Vague images were coming back to her, and suddenly the tiny cuts on her legs throbbed. The fundraiser. The drink. The immediate debilitating weakness.

"I survived." She shrugged. The words came out husky, strained. Like she hadn't spoken in a long time.

"Yeah."

Kita wracked her brain as the silence turned awkward. "Judge okay?" Not that she really cared.

"Yeah."

"Where am I?" Disappointment roared through her like an out-of-control raging river. She had let down Jill, and Hannah, and those kids.

"The judge's guest bedroom." Alex shifted his gaze so he wasn't looking at her. "I convinced him to take today off so you can rest and get back to fighting shape."

"Wait, so I'm still on the case?" She tried to connect the pieces but her synapses were firing at a sloth's pace, every movement, thought, like a slow-motion video.

"Of course you are."

But—

"You saved the judge." Alex barked. "And put your own life in danger."

Wasn't that what everyone expected?

"Jesus, Kita." Alex pushed up from the bed. "You aren't trained and you did a hell of a job under difficult circumstances."

Umm…"Thanks?" She had to say it again; this time it grated just a little less.

The silence continued. The room was slightly stale, as if the judge rarely had guests. At least not the kind who slept in the extra bedroom. The only thing saving her nose was the fresh clean scent of Alex's hair. How he could smell so fabulous when he'd clearly been asleep beside her was a good question. But filling her senses was that pine scent, like he'd just come from outdoors. His hair was all mussed, slightly curling behind his ears, as if maybe he needed a trim to keep himself all buttoned up. And God, she had to wonder what he'd look like if he totally let loose.

There was a tired cast to his eyes as he skimmed his gaze over her body. Looking for what she had no idea.

The gap in conversation started to become awkward. A tension invaded her limbs, because suddenly it occurred to her that she was in bed, wearing next to nothing, and he was next to her fully dressed. When his gaze dropped to her mouth, a flush she wasn't anticipating blossomed in her stomach, spreading outward, crawling up her chest and neck and into her face.

Even her ears burned.

A subtle tension shimmered between them.

She didn't know what to say to break this weird friction. He appeared on the verge of speaking.

The doorbell rang, interrupting the awkward moment.

Alex sprinted for the door as if the rules police were nipping at his heels. Sitting in bed with a fellow agent was probably a big fat no-no in his favorite book. "I'll be back."

Not sure if he meant to channel Arnold in the Terminator, but she was determined to at least be dressed when or if he returned.

She scrambled out from under the covers. In the corner was her small roller bag. She had another garment bag that held all the clothes from Jillian but the roller had her yoga and workout clothes and a nightgown. Which clearly no one had bothered to find.

She had another uncomfortable thought. Who had undressed her?

Digging through her bag, Kita yanked out yoga capris and a spandex halter top. She wished she had time for a shower; she smelled of antiseptic and hospital. When she bent her arm, the crook of her elbow twinged. She had another bruise on the back of her left hand, and the little cuts on her legs were stinging.

What had happened to her?

Carefully she eased the capri leggings over her cut-up shins.

Kita's mouth would qualify as a toxic waste facility so she hit the bathroom and quickly brushed her teeth. While she was getting cleaned up, her thoughts shifted to Hannah, who she'd promised to stay in touch with every day. Yesterday she'd only texted that she was working on a solution to her problems. She didn't want to get her hopes up before Jillian had a plan in place. But Kita needed to find her phone and at least touch base.

Three sharp knocks, almost bangs, hit the bedroom door.

"Come in."

Alex poked his head in but avoided her gaze. "Team meeting in five."

Huh. *Team.* She was part of the team now. Guess getting poisoned and almost killed upped her credibility. "I'll be right out."

ALEX FOUGHT the urge to pace the judge's ornate living room. At his current rate he'd wear a hole in the expensive wool rug.

Jillian Larsen was here, along with Shep, and some big dude who looked like the Rock's younger brother.

Kita strode into the room in skintight spandex, showing no weakness. If he hadn't had a ringside seat to her barely breathing medical emergency last night, he wouldn't believe she'd been unconscious the better part of twelve hours.

When she saw the giant who could bench yesterday's limo no problem, her entire face metamorphosed. Her lips and brows lifted, her cheeks widened, and her eyes sparkled. She practically threw herself at the Rock wannabe. "Hey, Dwayne."

Dwayne—really?—wrapped his overly large biceps around her head and pulled her in to his massive chest. "You okay?"

Her face was hidden from Alex's view, but her shoulders lifted. Dropped. "I'll live."

And thank God, or really Mila, for that.

"Good news," Dwayne said blandly. But there was relief in his eyes and his smile was blindingly white.

Emotion bubbled up inside Alex. Gratitude, annoyance, jealousy? He didn't like this proprietary urge that came over him whenever another man was touching her. It was none of his goddamn business who she wanted to wrap around like a layer of Saran Wrap. Her personal life was inconsequential to his mission and his job.

Still, he was honest enough with himself to acknowledge that his response was beyond a tepid "didn't like it." He hated that this Neanderthal was holding her.

So far the employees of Adams-Larsen did not resemble anyone he knew in public relations. "So I guess your PR clients need security?"

There was a silent, pregnant pause.

"We're a full-service agency," Jillian Larsen said

smoothly. "We offer whatever our clients need." The slight hesitation before she answered tugged at him, but they had bigger things to worry about.

"If we're all here," Alex clipped out. "Let's get started."

He strode down the hall to the judge's bedroom and rapped sharply on the mahogany paneled door.

The judge exited his room. His smarmy, nearly sleazy mask was firmly back in place.

Alex wanted to knock it askew and dig into what was beneath that slick exterior. The man was a federal judge, for fuck's sake. He had to be intelligent and wily and able to analyze situations for maximum potential and minimum risk. Not to mention Bobby Adams sat the bench for federal criminal cases, which meant he was fully versed with people who lied to save their own skin.

Dwayne had released Kita and she was smoothing down her hair. Her tumbled look sent Alex's thoughts straight where they shouldn't.

Her in that bed. The lacy black lingerie she'd worn beneath that stunning jade dress. And Jesus, she'd almost died, he needed to get over that.

"My dear." The judge sauntered to Kita's side and took her delicate hand in his. "Thank you. I'm so glad you will recover."

Her shudder was likely imperceptible to anyone else, but Alex was hyperaware of her mood. Her momentary happiness at seeing her coworker Dwayne evaporated when the judge touched her.

Since the threat to the judge had escalated and the health of Adams-Larsen's employee had been in peril, Alex's boss had insisted Jillian Larsen be kept in the loop. He still couldn't figure out why his boss was willing to accommodate and work with a woman who'd been a disgrace to the US

Marshals, but he wasn't in a position to question anything right now.

The judge had requested that Marsh Adams be present at this debrief and mission planning session but the former marshal was noticeably absent. Again.

"Is Marsh joining us?" The judge directed the question at Jillian Larsen.

Her lips tightened, infinitesimally, but Alex recognized her irritation. "He wasn't able to break away from his current assignment."

Which Alex might have believed if Kita hadn't also appeared strained. Just for a second. Something else was going on beneath the surface. But he couldn't imagine that Marsh Adams's absence had anything to do with the judge's situation, so he didn't care.

For some reason, the judge didn't go off on Larsen. But his disappointment was clear.

Kita's worried glance at Jillian Larsen confirmed something was going on with Marsh Adams.

They all sat at the large dining room table, a mahogany oval with a finished edge and a shiny dark stain. A long fabric rectangle adorned with orange pumpkins and golden cornucopia ran the length of a table that could seat twelve easily. Candlesticks and glittery fake pumpkins were scattered across the fabric. So either the judge had a girlfriend or a decorator. Based on the way he'd been pawing Kita last night, and the jealousy of his assistant, Alex's bet was on a decorator.

"What have you got?"

"Fingerprints on the bill were a nonstarter, just like we expected." Shep tapped the shiny wood tabletop. "Security cameras inside the ballroom and at the entrance didn't capture the woman giving the waiter the drink."

"How?" Alex barked out.

"There are some very small gaps, and apparently this woman knew to avoid them."

Jillian Larsen was all business. "Were we able to get pics of the crowd when the drink went flying? By the way, good work, Kita."

Dwayne patted her hand. "No one was paying undue interest to the waiter or the judge. My guess is she left, but by now she'll know her attempt failed."

"What about the waiter? Any luck getting him to identify the woman?" Kita rubbed her wrist.

"Dead end." Shep said, "We had him watch the footage but he didn't see the woman."

"So we need to be extra diligent from here on out." Alex wanted Dwayne's hand off Kita. "Any information on the tox screen?"

Shep continued, "The drink contained a high level of aspirin."

Jillian spoke. "Over the counter?"

Shep nodded. "Plain old, everyday aspirin."

Kita jerked. "How did we get that information so fast?"

"Doctor Patel swabbed your legs and had the lab use a quick response test to get a preliminary result. We'll get the full screen results in another twenty-four hours, but at least we have a starting point."

"What would aspirin do to you?" Kita's gaze had shifted to the judge.

"Almost kill *you*," growled Alex.

"Yeah, but that's me. While allergy to aspirin is relatively common, I happen to have an extremely severe reaction to it. But for most normal people, it wouldn't have made a blip in their health."

The judge had been uncharacteristically silent while they'd batted ideas back and forth.

"Why aspirin?"

The judge shifted uncomfortably in his ornately carved chair.

"Judge?" The steel in Alex's voice was necessary. He didn't typically talk to a protectee this way but the man had to be withholding information.

The judge cleared his throat, pressed his palms to the mahogany dining table, and stared at his hands. "I have a little problem with diabetes," he confessed.

Not a huge surprise, so did approximately ten percent of the United States population. "I'm missing something." Alex frowned.

"Aspirin can interfere with insulin levels. A high dose could possibly cause extremely low blood sugar," Judge Adams said reluctantly.

"So theoretically if you had that drink…."

"Well, the combination of alcohol, aspirin, and an empty stomach, since we hadn't eaten dinner yet, would have done some damage."

Done some damage. Alex was trying to wrap his brain around the judge's statement. "Would it have killed you?" he asked bluntly.

"I don't know." The judge had lost all his bluster. "Diabetes isn't an exact science. Everyone's body reacts differently. We'd have to ask my doctor, but even then he might not know the precise outcome of ingesting a large dose."

But the fact that someone had tried to give him aspirin seemed to suggest that the person had done in-depth research on the judge. "This indicates either personal knowledge or access to high-level intelligence."

The judge cleared his throat.

"How many other people know you have diabetes, Bobby?" Jillian Larsen insisted.

"Not many."

Alex put steel in his voice. "Ballpark it for us."

"Five, maybe six. My assistant, my bailiff, my ex-wife, me, my doctor, and likely his nurse, and my pharmacist."

That was a damn short list.

"Could any of them be compromised?"

"Everyone can be coerced," Kita said. "With the right incentive."

Jillian said, "We need more intelligence, Judge."

The older man blinked. Irritation washed over his features before he smoothed his face into a bland, smarmy mask.

Alex threw in the details from the marshals' official investigation. "The Office of Professional Investigation is also reviewing all his cases to see if anyone has recently gotten out of jail. If we narrow the pool down to women, it will go faster."

But Kita was shaking her head. "Vengeance. Could be the spouse or significant other that he put away, rather than the actual person."

"It's a level removed," Alex shot back.

"Possessive or violent behavior isn't relegated to just men," Kita said softly.

He didn't like the way she'd drawn into herself. And he definitely didn't like the way her boss was looking at her.

The judge had been stonewalling this investigation from the beginning. "Why did you request protection if you aren't going to be cooperative?" Alex kept his voice level, but Shep still shot a surprised look his way.

Yeah, as far as Alex knew, typically they weren't too rough on their judicial protectees.

The judge flushed, creeping up his ruddy face and turning him an even brighter shade of red. "I didn't."

"You...." Alex couldn't finish.

"My, ah, assistant, Vanessa, is the one who turned the letters over to the US Marshals Judicial Protection Service." The judge looked sheepish. "I didn't think there was a credible threat."

Alex was trying to wrap his brain around the fact that the judge had not been the one to request protection. And one thought kept returning to the forefront. "Then why did you ask for backup from Adams-Larsen?"

The silence in the room was overwhelming.

Kita responded, saving the judge. "Let's focus on the more pressing issue. Clearly the threat to the judge *is* real."

So, yeah, they needed to be focused on protecting the judge. But eventually he wanted to know why the judge had insisted on Adams-Larsen.

"And we need to game a security plan with the updated information." Jillian continued. "I'd like you to bring Dwayne in on this."

"No obvious bodyguards in public," the judge said gruffly.

So Alex's initial analysis had been correct. The judge didn't want anyone to know he was under protection.

The doorbell rang just as Shep's phone buzzed.

"Excuse me, this is the security for the building. I need to answer." Shep turned away from the table.

The judge stood, but Dwayne stepped in front of him. "Let's move to a more secure location."

Kita headed for the door along with Alex.

Shep was talking quietly. Alex listened to his partner's

conversation with one ear even as he focused on Kita. "I'll answer. You stand behind the door."

Kita's presence beside him sparked an unusual level of concern for her welfare.

"I've got training." She kept pace with him, trying to convince him she was capable.

"You were completely debilitated a few hours ago." Alex didn't want her anywhere near the door. "Let me handle it."

Shep had hung up. "Security cameras fritzed."

Alex stopped, stood to the side of the door in case someone was on the other side ready to unload a weapon. He unholstered his weapon and thumbed off the safety.

"The doors in this place are steel reinforced," Kita commented. "You're in more danger on the side of the door than behind it."

She stepped up to the door and peered through the security peephole. "No one."

Alex nudged her out of the way. Carefully, he turned the deadbolt and opened the door.

No one was there. Alex looked left, then right. The hallway was empty. He stepped out into the hall. The elevator was silent. The only other escape route was the stairway at the end of the hall.

Alex took off at a run. "Lock the door behind me."

Chapter 10

Kita hesitated for less than a second.

"Keep the judge under guard," she ordered the room at large.

She shot out the door after Saunders. Since he went right, she went left. But the end of the hallway was a dead end. There was no escape outlet this way. She headed back to the co-op. The short jog down the hallway had tired her out.

She leaned against the door frame and guarded the entrance to the judge's home. No one would get past her while she waited for Alex Saunders to return. It didn't take long.

He burst from the stairwell exit.

Frowned when he saw her. "What are you doing out here?"

"I went the other way." She jerked her head toward the end of the empty hallway.

"You were supposed to stay inside."

"Yeah, well…orders and I don't always mix." She held his stare, until he blew out a breath.

"We're going to talk about this." Then he did the chin lift.

"We're partners. I was just backing you up." She smirked. Good thing she pulled that out of her ass because she pretty much hadn't been thinking about Alex when she'd gone left.

His mouth twisted and she was pretty sure it wasn't with amusement, but action drew her gaze to his lips, which drew her mind to other less serious pursuits.

"Inside," he barked.

She had to stop having these feelings. Being inappropriately attracted to her "partner" had bad idea written all over it. And while she didn't always follow the rules, she did listen to her gut. Getting tangled up with Alex Saunders was a terrible idea. Kita dropped her gaze to the floor to hide the sudden flare of lust. That's when she saw an envelope on the floor.

Alex said, "Shit. Where did that come from?"

"No idea. I just noticed it." Kita bent down to grab it.

"Don't touch."

Fortunately, she'd already seen the white crystals on the beige carpet. Kita snatched her fingers back against her breastbone.

"You see that?" She glanced at Alex, dread filling her up because a letter for a federal judge and dusted with white powder was never a good sign.

Alex said, "Could be anthrax." He tucked his weapon in his holster and pressed a button on his phone. "We're going to need the HAZWOPER team at Judge Robert Adams's residence." He nodded, then hung up the phone.

He stared at her steadily. "So not all rules are off-limits?"

"I may be impulsive but I'm not stupid." Kita defended

her actions. "Look. The judge was adequately guarded inside his co-op." He wasn't going to rattle her.

"You agreed I was lead on this."

Kita fought a snarky comment. "True. But——"

"Let's just leave it at that. We need to focus on this more immediate problem right now. Later we can tackle your insubordination."

Okay, maybe he was going to rattle her. *Insubordination?*

Alex pressed another button on his phone. "Shep… Suspicious envelope at the judge's front door. Waiting for Hazmat. Keep everyone quarantined inside until we confirm there is no poison or threat."

She could hear Shep squawking through the phone line. He was still yakking when Alex disconnected the call. Alex leaned against the wall on the opposite side of the hallway. All the adrenaline that coursed through her earlier disappeared, and with a whoosh she slid to the floor. Back against the wall, legs propped, and elbows on her knees, she tilted her head back and closed her eyes.

"Hey, you okay?" The concern in his voice surprised her. That shadowy memory of him hovering over her, whispering that he wouldn't let anyone hurt her, slithered through her mind again.

The feelings he evoked were unfamiliar. She took care of herself. Even when she'd been kicked out of her mother's house and gone to live with Marsh and his mom when she'd been seventeen. "Yeah."

But maybe she'd overdone it a bit.

"Any specific symptoms? Shortness of breath? Rapid heart rate?" He'd perked up, his gaze scanning her for injury. He knelt down beside her. His unique piney scent invaded her consciousness, calming her rising anxiety.

"I'm good. But, ah—" Kita squirmed against the wall "—thanks for asking."

His blue eyes sparkled, lightening his features, and his mouth quirked. "That was pretty tough, huh?"

His entire demeanor shifted. Gone was the serious, severe rule follower. In his place was a guy intent on mischief.

"You should laugh more often." She spoke without thinking. Of course. And she wasn't even sure why she was giving him advice on laughing since she rarely managed that particular action herself.

Alex ignored her and punched in a number on his phone, then set it on the floor. The speaker blared as the phone on the other end rang.

Shep answered. "Gaffney."

"Any word on the cameras?"

"This floor, plus one above and one below had malfunctions."

Well that was fucking handy.

"Get the tapes of the entire building."

"Already on it."

Alex blew out a breath. "I'll call with an update once HAZWOPER gets here."

"Ten four." And Shep was gone, they were back to her and Alex. Alone.

With a packet of anthrax? She couldn't think about the implications of that.

"Pretty fucking bold." Kita stared at that envelope, wondering if they were at serious risk of being contaminated. She rubbed at the knob on her left wrist.

"Yeah, and the attacks are escalating."

"As if they knew he had protection?" Except the judge

had tried to keep that nugget a secret. Right now, Alex was posing as a driver and Kita as an aide.

Alex mulled that over.

His gaze followed her unconscious act of rubbing her wrist. Her tell. She knew it but most of the time it didn't matter. She spent her days in front of a computer screen or training clients in self-defense.

"What happened to your wrist?"

She stopped rubbing. "I followed the rules."

"What?"

Her gaze kept straying to that envelope. "What does HAZ-whatever stand for?" She rubbed her wrist again.

"Hazardous waste operations and emergency response team." Alex squatted down, clearly trying to put her at ease. "The CDC and the government have a strict emergency response protocol in place. It will be fine."

She blinked. Her eyes a gritty mess, makeup caked at the corners, reminding her that she'd been unconscious not too long ago. She couldn't afford to show any more weakness. "Okay."

"There's no need to panic."

"I'm not panicking." Not exactly. But holy shit, anthrax.

"We'll be given an antivax and started on a course of antibiotics and quarantined until they can figure out if the powder is actually a toxin."

Quarantined. With Alex Saunders. "How long?"

He shrugged. "I don't know."

"In the co-op?"

"Likely not. They haven't been exposed so they may quarantine them inside the apartment."

"Do you think that was the purpose?" Kita speculated. "If she—they—wanted to ensure that the judge was in a certain place, then the best way to do that is to trap him in a known area."

Alex considered her comments. Nodded. "Good point. But the response team still won't quarantine the people in the apartment with us."

Us. A shiver went over her spine. She was going to be trapped in a place with Agent Saunders. Weirdly that didn't upset her as much as it should.

The HAZWOPER team arrived, cutting off their conversation. Men and women in breathing masks, white jumpsuits, and anti-contamination gloves secured the area around the judge's door.

A doctor administered a shot to each of them.

They were given containment suits to get them out of the building, loaded into a secure van, and taken to a properly prepared facility trained to deal with an anthrax outbreak.

Through the exams and shots and questions, Kita's energy began to flag. She literally felt like she was wilting under the strain.

Hours later, they were finally ensconced in a US Marshals safe house not too far from downtown DC. The rowhouse was part of a long line of houses, in the middle of a slightly rundown neighborhood. The security alarm ensured that the house would stay undisturbed. Their defensive concerns were different from the regular ones associated with hiding and securing a federal witness. Mostly the Marshals just needed a place to stash them until the test results could confirm or deny the presence of anthrax in that letter.

The Marshals had moved the judge and the rest of the occupants of the co-op per Alex's instructions.

They'd also evacuated the judge's entire floor under the pretense of a building inspection finding potential black mold and needing to do a thorough cleaning before letting the inhabitants back in.

Alex ran his piece of the investigation from his cell phone, and Kita mostly twiddled her thumbs. She wasn't used to being superfluous and she didn't like it. She also didn't like the fact that she hadn't had a chance to talk to Jillian about Hannah and the kids. The worry that she'd woken up with hadn't diminished. If anything, she was more stressed. She'd promised to keep in touch with Hannah every day.

A wilted and browned violet plant sat on the windowsill behind the sink. Kita pinched off the brown leaves and poked at the dirt.

She tended to the plant, holding the green plastic pot beneath the water spigot and soaking the dry crunchy soil until it was saturated. Satisfied with the way the plant perked back up, she placed the pot on a paper plate and set it back on the sill.

"Sit on the sofa," Alex ordered. Wow, she must look bad. Had the infection begun taking effect?

That she could have that sickness in her swirling, poised to attack her body, hovered in the back of her mind like a leopard waiting to pounce.

Kita was feeling particularly battered and bruised. And the one thing she could do, the one place she had a semblance of control, was the situation with Hannah.

"You want something to eat?" Alex asked her.

"Not really hungry."

She heaved the Target bag with their supplies on her shoulder. "I'm going to go change."

Kita found the first bedroom and quietly closed the

door. She pulled off the scrubs that made her feel dirty, and pressed the speed dial on her phone, stripping off the rest of the clothes as she waited impatiently for Hannah to answer.

ALEX PEERED IN THE FRIDGE.

Something was off with his partner. He'd only known her for a day and a half but he was convinced that she was worried about something. The edgy, antsy feeling that gripped him in the hospital last night—or was it the night before?—was back. Stronger than ever.

He thought he heard Kita talking.

Was she okay?

He hustled to the sleeping area of the safe house in time to hear her rattle off her phone number. "Call me."

What the hell was she doing?

They didn't know if the judge's letter writer was doing surveillance. Clearly the perpetrator had intimate knowledge or access to the judge.

Accordingly, the team was supposed to maintain radio silence until they could get a handle on what was happening with the escalating threats.

He burst into her room. And stopped cold.

Kita had taken off the scrubs she'd been given. Her back was to him, and all he could see was miles of skin. Rippling, smooth, sensual skin. The muscles in her back, the dip of her waist, the rounded curves of her ass, and strong, sexy legs.

She was a fucking goddess.

Her head was tilted back as she stared at the ceiling. Her eyes were closed, one hand gripping the back of her neck,

99

the other hanging by her side with the cell phone still clutched in her elegant fingers.

"Close your mouth."

"What?"

"Perhaps you could get out," she said evenly.

He whirled around so that his back was to her. "Not yet."

"Really?" she groused. "I've had an epically bad few days. I would like to be left alone, for just a few damn minutes."

So had he. But he'd be lying if he hadn't been listening intently when they'd been trapped in that exam room and answering question after question of personal information.

She'd been exposed to TB as a kid, which meant she had potentially compromised lungs in the event that the powder was inhalation anthrax.

"Why aren't you gone?"

"I turned my back." And he had, but when he opened his eyes, he realized that she had turned around and he could see the front of her body reflected in the mirror over the dresser.

Shit. He squeezed his eyes shut again.

Kita's husky laugh penetrated his consciousness. "What's the matter?"

"Nothing," he groaned. His body had responded to the sight of all that skin; her small breasts were pert and tipped with peach nipples. The weather had turned chilly today and the house had not yet warmed up.

"Got a little peep show?"

"Would it help if I said I was sorry?"

"Maybe." She wasn't going to give an inch. "But I'd rather know why you burst in here."

His brain had shorted out. She'd wandered closer and

Alex was overly mindful of the fact that she didn't have a stitch of clothing on. The thatch of dark curls at her sex didn't match her hair, a fall of color that started dark at the roots but ended blond at the tips. Logically this made sense, but the stark contrast pulled at his concentration. He wondered what she tasted like. Wondered if her whole body exuded that sexy citrus scent. Wondered what she'd sound like if he kissed her in other more intimate places.

He remembered her soft moan from the other evening, remembered the lust that had possessed him, and the caution he'd abandoned at the first sign of her aggression when she bit his lip. He swiped his tongue over the still sensitive curve.

She waited for his answer patiently.

What was the question? More importantly, did he care? Because other more dangerous, tempting desires were rising in his body.

He was only steps away from her. From her gorgeously *naked* body.

And her completely hidden thoughts.

The fact that they'd potentially been exposed to a deadly toxin, that if it manifested would begin with flulike symptoms and erode their immune system until they either died or recovered, churned in his gut.

All those rules followed, all those strict interpretations of right over wrong, so that no one got hurt, people stayed safe. And he still ended up here.

On the edge of extinction.

"Put on some clothes, Kita."

She laughed huskily. "Or what?"

In that moment, his only cogent thought was survival. Survival of his own DNA. Yes, it was primitive, and no, right in this fucking moment, he didn't care.

"Do you really want to find out?"

His cock had stiffened, pressing against the scrubs insistently. He opened his eyes, caught her gaze in the mirror. She knew he had been staring at her. She knew he was aroused. Kinda hard to miss.

Her gaze dropped to the significant bulge beneath the rough blue cotton. Held, as if mesmerized by the wood he was sporting.

Her nipples pebbled.

"That for me?" she said seductively.

Hell yes it was for her. "Do you see anyone else in this room?"

She licked her lips and all he could imagine was them wrapped around his cock and sucking him dry.

"Fuck, Kita." His voice was like grated glass. "Put some damn clothes on."

Instead she took a step toward him. "Or you could take yours off," she offered.

All the blood in his brain rushed to his cock. He was harder than he'd ever been in his life. Hemoglobin and antibodies flooded his body and the club in his pants throbbed painfully.

The chill air in the sparse, impersonal room cooled the sheen of sweat on his skin but did nothing to cool his epic stiffy. His body was an inferno of lust.

Her nipples peaked, just begging for his hands, his mouth.

She took another step. "We have nothing to do but wait."

The results of the analysis should be in sometime tomorrow, two days at the latest. Until then they were in a state of nothingness. Poised on the edge. Depending on the identity of that powder they were in for a wild ride to survival. Or they would breathe in relief at the deadly bullet they'd dodged.

"I don't really want to lie around and worry." Kita was right behind him now. Heat pulsed off her body in waves. This close he could see her arousal. The flush in her breasts and the glitter of desire in her black eyes.

He tried to remind himself of all the reasons why this would be monumentally bad.

"I make my own rules," she said softly. "And my rule says when you've been exposed to a deadly toxin, you grab hold of every moment you can. Because nothing is ever guaranteed, and no matter how much you plan and do everything right, things can go terribly, horrifically wrong."

Wasn't that what he'd been thinking just moments ago?

Nothing was certain in this world. Undoubtedly not tonight.

Her gaze had dropped to his erection again. This close, her delicate scent and the faint musk of arousal drifted to him. "So this isn't just a convenience?"

Sex usually meant something to him. He had a set pattern he adhered to. A series of steps that were typically taken before he actually went to bed with a woman.

"Jesus, Alex." She dropped her forehead to his shoulder. "You seriously have rules for sex too?"

As if she knew him.

"Maybe," he said defensively. Then screw it. "But I've wanted you since I saw you in Jillian's office."

"I was all sweaty and I smelled."

"I know."

Her mouth rounded in a surprised O.

"Fuck your rules." She carefully set the phone on the dresser and stepped in front of him. She stared into his eyes, very deliberately clasped his hands and dragged his palms to her bare breasts, pressing them against her.

She placed her own hands over his erection, rubbing up and down the hard length until a drop of liquid wet the scrubs.

"And fuck me," she commanded him.

Chapter 11

K ita could literally feel the moment he broke.
He'd been standing still as her Buddha statue.
Not moving and even though the heat from his swollen cock
was burning through the blue scrubs he wasn't doing a
damn thing about it.

She'd been a humiliating moment away from dropping
her hand and walking away.

Not running away in shame, but for damn sure slinking
away in disappointment.

And then he'd groaned.

His palms squeezed her tits and his thumbs pressed hard
against her nipples. All that pent-up arousal thrummed
through her.

She moaned low in her throat.

That galvanized him.

The imbalance of naked vs. clothed probably should
have bothered her. Instead she leaned into the heat of his
body, reveled in his hard cock against her belly. Kita slid her
hands beneath the elastic waist and cupped his ass in her
palms.

Alex caressed her breast with one hand while the other snaked around her waist and slid along her skin until his fingertips rested at the top of her ass.

His finger teased the valley between her ass cheeks even as he bent to kiss her.

His lips were soft but the kiss was hard, frenetic, invasive. She nipped at his mouth and he opened. Kita thrust her tongue inside in short strokes. Her hips rocked in the same rhythm as the dance of their tongues. She wanted to get him naked. Get skin to skin, but his callused fingers were playing with her nipple, and sensation after sensation crashed through her, shorting out her motor function.

All she could do was feel.

He devoured her, as if she was his last meal, a banquet, and he'd been starving to death.

She shoved the scrub shirt up and over his head, breaking their kiss. He dragged his nose along the curve of her neck, goose bumps shivering over her bare skin. "How can you still smell so good?"

She licked a path across his chest, stopping to play with his nipple.

His erection busted out of the waist of the pants and a smear of hot liquid sizzled on her belly. They were both breathing heavily, even though she'd done little more than kiss him and run her hands over his bare flesh.

Damn, he had a spectacular body. She closed her eyes and skimmed her tongue over his washboard abs, tasting each ridge like a feast of her very own muscle buffet. His skin was slightly salty and he smelled like a man. Like pine and male sweat and sweet arousal.

She shoved his pants down his thighs to his knees. Then she dipped to push them to the ground. She was half kneeling, and his engorged cock was in her face. He jutted hard and thick and eager from the nest of curls and she had the urge to suck him into her mouth. The bulbous head of his cock was swollen and purple, and the vein that ran down the front beckoned.

Her mouth watered but before she could consume him, he yanked her to her feet, then whirled them around.

With deliberate steps he walked them to the simple bed with the plain comforter.

Her calves hit the box spring, and she tumbled to the mattress.

Alex paused, stared, his gaze hot licks over her skin. Her sex was wet, tingling with anticipation as he knelt and skimmed his thumbs up the inside of her thighs. He stopped at the crease in her leg, rubbed his thumbs along her skin, edging ever closer to her swollen sex, but not quite touching. His breath was hot on her clit as he bent over and took one long, slow lick.

"Goddamn, you taste amazing." He spoke against the lips of her sex and then his head dove between her thighs and he began to eat at her in earnest.

His stubble prickled the overly sensitive skin of her inner thighs.

She typically wasn't crazy about guys going down on her. It seemed so self-indulgent, and she went to stop him.

Alex's eyes were closed but the expression of bliss on his face cracked open something inside her. Her heart hiccupped. He wasn't enduring this as foreplay. His cheeks were flushed and his smile as he lapped at her was the same one he'd had when she'd told him he should laugh more often. He was enjoying this.

"Relax, Kita." He growled against her, the low sound shimmying through her body. He wrapped one arm around her thigh and lifted her higher. Then he skated two fingers along the back of her thigh, and a cascade of tingles buzzed through her.

Her hips began to rock and instead of trying to get away, she ached to get closer. The things his mouth were doing to her were probably illegal.

Then he pressed those fingers against her aroused and swollen flesh before gliding inside her easily as if he'd penetrated her a thousand times.

His confidence, the ballet of his movements as he slipped right in and stroked with a masterful touch, was a total panty-melter. He had a plan and he wasn't afraid to follow it.

His fingers pushed inside—not rough but not gentle—stroked, probed, and then he found that spot.

"What is that?" she gasped. Dear God, his fingers were playing her like a fucking violin.

"I am a G-man." He grinned, her juices glistening in his stubble.

Without warning he sucked her clit into his mouth and relentlessly pushed her toward implosion. He ate at her, his fingers punished her, and then he used his other hand to pinch her clit.

Her legs tightened around his face as involuntary jerks of her hips pushed her into his fierce desire.

She came in a long, loud wail, bowing off the bed as if she could push her pussy into his mouth and have him swallow her whole. Her sex milked his fingers, greedy and grasping for something, anything, to hold on to. The contractions were so hard, higher thought was impossible.

Fireworks rocketed in her head, blinding her. With his smooth shoulders practically underneath her ass and her legs pushed wide open for his onslaught, sensation overwhelmed her.

Sex wasn't like this. This all-consuming battery of the senses, taking away basic impressions and leaving only sated, wrecked, throbbing parts in its wake.

She'd had sex, many times. She used it like a tool when she wanted some stress relief. But those tepid orgasms were nothing like what just plowed through her body.

He continued to eat at her sex, and her over-sensitized body protested. She couldn't take any more. She need to get away from the overwhelming lust that clawed at her, annihilating feelings that welled up, crowding her throat. She couldn't handle what was happening.

She did a sit up and tugged on his hair.

His clean-cut, Mr. Upstanding, By the Book image was in tatters.

He hadn't shaved today, a dark scruff covered the lower half of his face, giving him a decidedly more disreputable appearance. His chest was a work of muscled glory, his biceps bunched with tension, his hair stood up in spikes from where she'd clenched the strands in her fists. His lips and mouth and cheeks were slick from her orgasm. She'd come all over his face.

With a growl, she pulled him on top of her, wrapped her legs around his waist and rolled him until she was on top.

"My turn." Here was a position she was comfortable assuming.

She was in control. She was directing the action and his pleasure. Because she knew for now her satisfaction was over.

He grinned. Those white teeth were blinding in the dim room. "Whatever you want, sweetheart."

Her heart clenched at the term of endearment.

His cock pulsed against her wet sex. He shifted his hips and the bulbous head played with her clit.

Still sensitive, she held in a gasp. "Condom?"

That quickly his smile disappeared. "I don't have one."

She thought back to that room where they'd been disinfected and quizzed on their current health. She'd overheard every single detail of his physical history, including the results of his annual exam for the US Marshals. "No diseases."

"I never go without." His hands gripped her hips. He was slowly rocking her back and forth over his erection. Big, hard, hot, he continued to tease and torment her with the slippery head. And oh God but she wanted him inside her.

The desire she'd thought sated was quickly rising again. Impossible. And yet, she couldn't stop those subtle caresses, teasing him right back.

"Me either." She dropped her head, arching her back, trying sort of to get away from him, but he wouldn't let her lift from that seductive, teasing tip. "I have an IUD," she whispered, unsure if she wanted him to take her up on the unspoken offer.

Then she remembered the little bag of toiletries the hospital staff had given them. "What about the bag from the hospital?"

"Please God. Yes!" Her bag was on the pillow where she'd tossed it before she called Hannah. Kita snatched it up and dug through cache of toothpaste, mouthwash, shampoo, and conditioner until she found the little wrapper.

Triumphantly she held the packet between her fingers.

Alex wrapped his hand around her wrist. "Tell me what you want."

He was leaving it up to her. She wanted him. Wanted his cock. Wanted him to fuck her into tomorrow.

Actions speak louder than words. She ripped open the package.

Hell, they were potentially exposed to a deadly toxin. They could start showing signs of illness as soon as twelve hours from now. She would never forgive herself, or him, if she didn't take this moment.

"I need you to say it."

"Fuck." She rolled the condom over his engorged penis.

"Fuck what?" he grated out. Clearly willing to stop if she put on the brakes.

"Me." Kita pushed against his hold, bearing down on his cock. "Fuck. Me."

With that final permission, he slammed her down on his cock so hard her swollen sex bumped up against his abdomen.

The root of his cock hit her clit, sending a zing of pure lust through her.

"Holy shit." He split her in two, and made her whole.

She grabbed his forearms and the muscles in his biceps bulged when he lifted her and slammed her back down again.

He'd taken her at her word. This was no tender sweet sex. This was pure fucking. Lost in the intensity of their connection, he gripped her hips so hard she was going to have bruises, and a crazy thrill went through her.

Alex shoved up inside her, the head of his cock massaged her G-spot with every thrust and slide until her head swam. It was supposed to be his turn but instead she was ramped up again and headed toward another orgasm.

Her breasts bobbed in his face and he curled up and took a nipple into his hot mouth.

It was too much, the pinch of his cock rubbing her clit with every thrust as if he wanted to slam inside her and have her hold him there.

His face was strained, his muscles corded and his cock,

dear God his cock just got bigger and bigger inside her. Her channel was full, spread wide. She felt exposed, open, vulnerable. And yet so fucking powerful.

Until he bit on her nipple and shoved her over the edge, screaming.

Her orgasm slammed into her as she went into a spinning freefall. Her sex spasmed around his cock in hard, powerful pulls, the contractions so intense her vision blacked. She shattered into a million pieces, so fragmented she could barely remember to breathe.

But her orgasm triggered his, and with a loud roar he poured himself into her body. His cock banged against her walls as his come jetted so hard she swore to God she could feel the pulses hitting her cervix.

Slick with sweat, she collapsed on top of him.

His arms went around her back. Their groins still interlocked like perfect puzzle pieces, everything inside her buzzing, her body swimming in a tide of satisfaction. She buried her face in the curve of his neck.

Their scents mingled together in a perfect perfume.

And the tension she'd been carrying, since they found the envelope that had sent them into solitary confinement, eased. At least for now.

He was still semi-hard inside her.

And when he rocked his hips up, her insides began tingling again. That…that wasn't possible. Yet with every little pulse of his hips, his pubic bone rubbed her clit and, unbelievably, sensations began to build again.

Alex slipped his hands around to her ass, rubbing one finger long the deep valley between the cheeks while his cockhead rubbed at her swollen, over-stimulated G-spot. He pressed his finger just a little closer to that puckered rosette and pushed her over the edge again.

Little tremors cascaded through her like a waterfall as the mini orgasm spread out through her body and fizzed in her brain.

"Jesus, you're a freaking sex god," she muttered against his neck.

His chest puffed, likely with pride. "When a job needs to be done…give it to the US Marshals."

She snorted. "You left out the 'and you don't know who to give it to' part."

"Well clearly you already knew who to give the job to."

He lifted her arm. Kita let it hang limply, too wrecked to move, or protest. He shifted, angling his head, and pressed an openmouthed kiss to the small tattoo that decorated the inside of her arm.

"What does this mean?"

"It's the symbol for strength in Chinese."

"Why?"

She rubbed at her wrist, remembering the day it was broken. The day her mother had broken her.

Chapter 12

S he'd wrecked him.

Alex savored her weight on top of his body. They were still intertwined, and they'd have to move soon, but right now he'd take this intimacy. And that was a little weird because he shouldn't feel this way. They barely knew each other.

They didn't agree on anything. Total opposites in every way that mattered.

Except she'd turned him inside out. And turned him on in a sexy, spontaneous and unexpected manner.

She rubbed her wrist again, and he pressed a line of kisses from her tattoo down her forearm. He clasped her wrist lightly and kissed the uneven bump, silently waiting for her explanation. He knew when not to push.

She sighed.

"Let's just say my mother and I had a…difference of opinion."

Her mother? "About what?"

"She was pissed I didn't get in to Princeton. Or Yale. Or Harvard."

He frowned, tensed. Wasn't sure how to proceed, which was unusual for him. "You said you broke it because you followed the rules."

"Yup." She laughed but it was a bitter, subdued sound. "I took all the right classes, volunteered at all the right charities, played three instruments, spoke four languages, wrote killer essays, and it still wasn't enough for me to get in to an Ivy League university."

"So where did you go?"

"MIT."

Massachusetts Institute of Technology? "Hardly a slacker school."

"According to my mother—a half-Vietnamese, half Chinese Tiger mom long before the media became outraged by what they considered harsh demands on kids—the only schools that matter are the Ivies." She held up her arm, stared at that knob, avoided his gaze. "She...beat the shit out of me."

His arms tightened around her. He'd disappointed his parents occasionally, especially when his brother had gotten hurt and he'd finally understood that rules were in place for a reason.

He still hadn't gotten over his brother's injuries and the harm he'd done to Drew. And yet even on that day, Alex could never in a million years imagine them hitting him. "Jesus." He wanted to shield her from future harm. "What about your dad?"

She tensed on top of him. "He died when I was about twelve."

He squeezed her closer, wishing for an odd moment that he could take away her grief. "I'm sorry. So what did you do?"

Because there was no way this tough, take-charge

woman hadn't taken action. She was a special brand of fearless.

"Moved out once I got out of the hospital." Kita pressed a kiss to his neck.

"Where did you go?"

"I moved in with Marsh and his mom."

"So that's how you know the unofficial slogan of the marshals?"

"Marsh Adams has been my friend for a long time."

"I'm glad he was there for you." Alex thought of all the ways that things could have been worse. Her positions on life became clearer. "So that's why you don't like the rules?"

"I'm sure a shrink would have a field day with me."

Silence lingered in the suddenly tense room. Because even though he could understand why she made her own rules, Alex followed the rules. He'd learned just the opposite. His brother had paid a terrible price because Alex hadn't wanted to listen. He'd learned a valuable lesson. They would never agree on this subject.

Could he make her understand?

"When I was young, I disobeyed the rules at camp. My brother followed me into the river and almost drowned. He got swept away, hit the rocks, broke his arm in three places."

Alex thought back to that day. The shame he'd felt when they found out he'd been the one to go in the river. It had been so hot at camp and all he'd wanted to do was cool off his feet. Remorse was a constant companion.

"Where were the counselors?"

"They were getting our lunch."

"You do realize that they bore the biggest responsibility."

He remembered the fear, then the disappointment on his mother's face. She'd given him the same lecture she always gave. *Follow the rules so you stay safe.* Yet, until the near tragedy happened, he really hadn't understood. Her words finally had meaning. And Alex had vowed to never again break the rules. In fact, he tended to have rules in place for everything. Rules kept people safe. They worked. In his job and in life.

"I disobeyed and people got hurt. If I'd listened, my brother would have been safe."

Kita snorted a breath against his neck. "Some rules are stupid."

He bristled.

She did a push-up and disconnected their bodies. The loss of her heat let in the frigid air, the loss of her body keenly defined in the suddenly awkward room.

He wanted to pull her back on top of him, reestablish that surprising intimacy. He wasn't ready to let go of her yet. But the wish stuck in his throat. She sauntered to the adjoining bathroom with tension vibrating her body, her muscles delineated, until all that was left was the vision of Kita's bare ass as she shut the bathroom door.

The phone on the dresser rang, shaking Alex out of his odd musings.

That was Kita's phone. He launched himself at the phone. They needed to turn it off. But by the time he got to the dresser, her cell was silent again.

Kita came barreling out of the bathroom still naked as the day she was born.

Her pert breasts bounced as she lunged for her cell. "Give me that."

Her anxiety set off loud warning signals.

"Who did you call earlier?" He held the phone high so that she couldn't reach it.

The air in the room cooled with her attitude. Her face

closed up tighter than the security at the White House. "No one who has anything to do with this job."

"Everything has to do with this job," he countered. He clenched his empty fingers into a fist balled at his side, and tried desperately to keep his gaze on her neck and above. But her stance was borderline combative and suddenly it was imperative that he know who she left that message for.

"I am not going to do anything to jeopardize the judge's safety."

"Then turn off your phone."

She shook her head, "I can't do that." She stood there, completely naked, and totally defiant. No shame, and a total lack of modesty that was somehow confusing. Her defiance underlined her refusal to be embarrassed.

"Kita, we need to be off grid."

"The judge isn't with us," she argued. "We're peripheral tonight."

Alex felt the familiar rush of frustration every time she subverted his rules. "You are blatantly ignoring my command."

"Let me see who called."

"Only if you promise to stop trying to contact them."

"Once I make sure she's all right."

"She?"

Kita's mouth tightened into a flat line.

"Who is she?"

"She has nothing to do with the investigation."

But that didn't answer his question. "Who?"

He felt ridiculous, like he was playing a game of keep-away on the playground. Except they weren't children and they were very naked. His cock was still sticky from their sexual encounter. And was totally on board with going for round two.

"She's a friend who's going through a rough time right now." She finally gave him some information. "Let me make sure she's okay."

Alex continued to study her. Wondering why this couldn't wait. Why she was so willing to flaunt her lack of respect for his request. But she wasn't backing down.

He watched the shift happen. When she didn't get her way by begging, she modified her tactics. Kita stepped into his personal space, so close her nipples brushed his chest. She tilted her head to the side and smiled sexily. Her eyes sparkled before she slowly ran her tongue along the center of his chest, up his neck until she nipped at his chin.

His cock didn't care that she was only using her sexual wiles to get the phone. He was on board with whatever Kita did next, rising to poke her in the stomach.

Alex needed to control the situation, which was rapidly spinning out of control. She rubbed her tits against his chest, and he groaned. "You aren't playing fair."

Because sure as shit, all she really wanted from him right now was her phone. His body wanted so much more and his mind was fascinated to watch her move, to see what she would do next. To see how far she was willing to go to get what she wanted.

"I play to win," she murmured against his beating heart.

Before he could step back, she slid down his body, slowly scraping her teeth along the ridges in his abdomen, before pausing at the head of his jutting cock. She lowered her head and sucked him into her mouth.

The heat and suction caused him to react right away. His cock swelled to bursting again, which should be impossible after the fucking they'd just done.

But he didn't want her this way.

Alex sighed.

Okay, maybe his dick would take her anyway it could. But he couldn't wrap his brain around the issue, like she was wrapped around his cock, sucking him hard, swallowing him down so that he penetrated her mouth all the way to the back of her throat. That tight constriction strangled his growing dick, and his body responded accordingly.

Then she moaned, the sound vibrating around his length in erotic stimulation.

"Stop." Alex dropped his arm, and rested the palm of the hand not holding the phone on her hair. "Jesus, I'll give you your phone back."

She released his cock with an audible pop. Her lips were swollen and canted up in a smirk as she held out her hand. "I would have finished you."

A flush pinkened her plump breasts, the tight points of her nipples revealing she was as aroused as he was.

"I'd rather finish together."

Which was true, and not. He hated that she was willing to do anything to get her phone back. And yet, his dick had loved the attention.

She dropped her gaze to his engorged and throbbing cock. "We'll see."

Alex handed the phone to her. Kita turned around, presenting her back. Her sleek muscles rippled enticingly.

Once again, he watched her reflection in the mirror. Quickly, she listened to the message.

Her eyes crinkled. The taunting little smile long gone from her expression.

Apprehension clouded her face as she clicked the end button on her phone. Alex had listened unashamedly but he'd only caught a few words. *Fine. Don't call. I'm fine.*

Kita's tight, closed expression caused him to ask again. "Who is she?"

"No one to concern yourself about."

Frustration bled from him. "I want to help."

"I get that." Kita pressed her lips together. "And I appreciate it, but you can't."

She wasn't going to tell him more.

She put her phone deliberately on the dresser and turned around. Her gaze going to his semi-wilted cock.

She stepped into him, her right hand reached beneath him and cupped his balls, rolling them around her fingers, while her left wrapped around his quickly reviving cock and squeezed.

Alex let her distract him from their problems. Because, after all, he wasn't an idiot.

Chapter 13

From somewhere off to her left, her phone rang. The shrill old-fashioned ringtone was sharp in that fuzzy place between sleep and awake.

Alex was already out of bed and reaching for the phone. *Hannah!* Kita jumped up.

Alex was speaking calmly into the cell. "Uh-huh. Uh-huh."

Was that her phone? She wasn't panicked exactly, but what the hell?

"See you in a few."

Alex clicked the off button and tossed the phone back on the dresser. His. Not hers.

"It was Shep." Alex snatched up the scrub bottoms from the bedroom floor. Last night's mistake was strewn over the carpeting like beer bottles from a frat party.

Kita tried not to flush when Alex tossed her panties at her.

"Not anthrax."

Tension flew out of her body in a whoosh of relief.

"What—" she cleared her throat. "What was it?"

Alex tugged his shirt over his head and ran his fingers through his disheveled hair, trying to put himself back together after last night's romp. "Splenda."

Thank God.

"So we're clear." Alex headed for the door. "Shep, Dwayne, and the judge will be here in two hours."

"Here?" So they were stuck here?

"The consensus was to move the judge into a more secure location." Alex paused, looked over her shoulder at the rumpled bed. "We've got the day shift. Shep and Dwayne have the night shift."

They were going to continue to work together. Usually Kita didn't care if she saw her sexual partners again. The act was intimate and yet usually a certain distance opened up between her and her conquest after they did the deed.

But with Alex, he brought up emotions and feelings that she'd like to forget.

And forget was exactly what she wanted regarding last night. That weird connection that wrapped around them in bed was false, like a glittering lure to an unsuspecting fish. She wanted to believe there was a happy ending at the tip of the hook. She couldn't count on that, because if life had taught her one thing, it was that people you got close to let you down.

It was only a matter of time. Better to not get too attached in the first place.

She rubbed her wrist. Forget that she'd bared far more than her body to this temporary lover.

She'd told him about her mother.

What the hell had she been thinking?

She flushed again.

"They're bringing over our bags."

"Good. Great. Well…" Ugh. She had no idea what to

say to him. He wouldn't meet her gaze, so she guessed he was as clueless and uncomfortable about how to proceed as she was. There weren't any rules to follow regarding what had just happened. So she would have to make up her own.

For a moment, she wanted that closeness back. Wanted to shelter in his embrace and hope for that connection to grow.

A hollow pit opened in her stomach, expanding in an ever-growing blob and threatening to swallow her whole. Of course he was backing away. People let you down. If her own mother couldn't stand her, why would she think anyone else would stick by her?

"Yeah." Alex opened the bedroom door. "I'll make breakfast."

With a quiet click, he shut the door.

And that was that. She should have known better than to carry around that hope even for a few minutes. Her focus needed to stay on keeping the judge safe so she could make sure Hannah and her nieces were taken care of. She wasn't going to let Hannah Smith down.

She couldn't believe that for a few minutes, she'd lost sight of her true goal. Saving Hannah Smith, protecting the judge, were what mattered. Not some tenuous and ephemeral thread between her and Alex. A thread she'd likely imagined.

Kita shrugged off her unease. She didn't have time to deal with unruly emotions and unexpected attractions. She picked up her cell and went into the bathroom.

Furtively she dialed Hannah's number.

No answer. Kita's gut twisted. Even though Hannah had said she was fine, Kita was pretty sure she'd been lying. She didn't like Frank Donner's escalation of violence. Jill had to come through with help soon.

ALEX SHUFFLED through the house to the next bedroom. He scrabbled through the drawers and found an unopened disposable razor and a small can of shaving cream. He laid out the razor, shaving cream and hand towel in a neat row, following his daily shaving ritual.

When he looked in the mirror, he felt as if something was out of focus, like a fuzzy filter on his phone he couldn't quite get into clarity. His scruff had gone from minimal to full-on scraggly. A stranger stared back at him. He was changing, had already changed. And he didn't like it.

Deliberately, Alex followed his shaving routine, scraping away the excess hair. He just wished he could cut away the sensation that everything was changing and that he wasn't going to be able to stop it.

After his shower, he pulled on a pair of sweats from the Target bag.

Pulling the fleece over his skin reminded him of Kita taking off the scrubs last night.

She'd seared him with her sexual exploration. But the true heat had come when she'd told him about her mother.

Her shame was apparent in the way she avoided his gaze and the bitter laughter she'd used to disguise her hurt.

He'd like a few minutes with her mom to talk about the proper way to treat your children.

His mother had smothered him with love, trying to drown out the remorse and guilt he'd lived with since the accident. His brother's outlook on life had shifted that day, and not for the better. Alex was filled with guilt every time his brother pulled some new crazy stunt.

But now was not the time or the place to lament his inability to control his surroundings.

So he headed to the kitchen to start breakfast, and considered the next steps in how to track down the person threatening the judge.

An hour later, Alex got a call on his cell.

Shep, Dwayne, and the judge were about five minutes out.

Kita was in the living room, on the raggedy shag carpeting that looked like it dated back to the seventies, curled up like a pretzel with her eyes closed and her palms resting on her knees. Bare in patches and folded in wrinkles, the carpet was a trip wire waiting to happen.

She was so still, only her chest moving in and out indicated she was breathing, but he didn't think she was aware of her surroundings. He stepped into the doorway between the kitchen and living area.

Her face had settled into a serene expression, but there was a little crinkle between her brows. Alex took the moment to study her. The sleek muscled arms and the delicate collarbones peeked from the deep V of the too-big T-shirt that nearly obscured her small breasts—except for the buds of her nipples, which stood out clearly against the simple cotton.

His mouth watered as he remembered sucking her into his mouth. Her sweet moans and her obvious pleasure when he inflicted the sensual pain.

He remembered her arching up into his thrusts, meeting him with pleasure and abandon. Equal partners in their sensual exploration. Her uninhibited responses to sex caused his cock to rise. Shit. Not the time to get an erection.

"You want something or are you just going to stare at me all day." She'd gone on the offensive, not afraid to address the attraction that boomeranged between them. But she still hadn't opened her piercing black eyes.

"Shep and Dwayne are bringing the judge in," Alex said. "I need you to watch the back of the house while I keep an eye on the front."

Kita lifted her lids. Her mouth pursed, but she didn't say a word.

Alex tried not to remember those puckered lips wrapped around his cock. And still his semi sported into full-on wood.

Shit.

Her gaze dropped to the tent in his sweats. "Okay." She unfolded gracefully from the lotus position and headed toward the back of the house.

Within a few minutes, Shep and Dwayne had hustled the judge through the back door.

Kita returned from her lookout. She nodded to everyone but stayed silent.

They all moved into the dining room. A scarred wood table had likely been picked up at Goodwill and four mismatched folding chairs were the only furniture in the bare room.

"You weren't followed?" After the two "sort of" attempts on the judge's life, which had backlashed on Kita, Alex wanted to make sure she was protected.

Shep gave a long suffering sigh. "No. We took the standard precautions."

Kita stood by the doorway, keeping herself slightly apart from everyone else. Alex's attention split between the table and the doorway.

"There's been no more activity or attempt to make contact." Dwayne rumbled from the head of the table.

Good, then they needed to get down to business and figure out who the hell was after the judge.

"I still think this is unnecessary." The judge blustered.

The four security consultants surrounded Judge Adams.

They needed answers. So far the attempts to harm the judge had been innocuous but the increased frequency indicated an escalation. The attacks could turn violent at any time. The judge needed to fess up.

Kita, who had been silent, turned to Dwayne. "You bring the laptop?"

Dwayne reached into an overly large messenger bag. "Here you go."

Alex's stomach grinded as Dwayne winked at Kita.

Her smile was radiant, and far too friendly. Alex wanted to beat his fucking chest and howl like a gorilla making his displeasure known and staking his claim.

"Yes," she said. "I'll start working to trace the online threats."

"We've got someone working on that," Alex pointed out.

"DON'T CARE if you have an entire division on the judge's letters." Kita had been attacked two days in a row and she wanted some damn answers.

"They aren't Kita," Dwayne said. His obvious praise soothed her, evening out her unsteady emotions. Sleeping with Alex Saunders had not been on her radar, and the feelings he'd evoked made her uncomfortable. Really uncomfortable.

She hated feeling vulnerable because she'd let him in.

She never shared the story about her mother. It was a defining moment in her life, changing the trajectory of her future. Far too personal to reveal to a lover. She needed to get her outer mask, her armor back in place before Alex thought she was weak, and prime for taking advantage of.

Kita shook off the unwanted vulnerability and rubbed

her hands together.

"What exactly do you do for Adams-Larsen?"

"I seed social media for maximum positive coverage."
Among other things.

"Social media?" Alex didn't disguise his scorn.

"Facebook, Twitter, SnapChat, Instagram, whatever."
She used random accounts to create a false trail to cover the
true movements of their clients. She also took over their
accounts to post updates on foursquare and other location
platforms to hide their true location.

ALIAS also used her skills when they had an actual
public relations client who needed some positive posts to
counteract previous negative engagement, realigning search
engine results to show positive and move the negative to
page two or even further down in the results.

"That isn't really what we need." The derision in Shep's
comment struck a nerve.

"I've got other skills." She hated the defensiveness that
rose within. "You guys get started with the questions while I
see what I can find out."

Kita ignored the look Alex shot at her and relaxed into
her comfort zone. The feel of the keys beneath her fingers
settled her. Here she was the queen. She knew what she was
doing, how to finesse information from high-tech
connections, pulling intel through the tentacles of the
information highway. But as she logged online, she was
acutely attuned to everyone else in the room.

The keys clacked loudly as she set up the tracking
software on her laptop to trace the email origins of the
threatening notes. But of course, finding the original
transmission point wasn't going to be that easy. It appeared
that the emails had bounced around, being fed through
several servers before being delivered to the judge.

"Do you have the list of women you've been involved with in the past year?" Alex asked.

"Is this really necessary?" The judge's surprisingly stark black eyebrows scrunched into a V over his vibrant blue eyes.

Weirdly, Kita thought he spent an extra second staring at her.

Alex must have picked up on it too because he shot her a questioning look.

She shrugged. She had no idea why the judge would look at her funny.

"Twice in the last two days someone has gotten close enough to hurt you if they wanted to. We need to get a handle on everyone you have been…involved with."

The judge sighed, long and loud. "If you insist." He drummed his big-boned fingers on the scratched up tabletop. "Grab some paper, this may take a bit."

Everyone paused. The level of anticipation had ramped up as they looked at her expectantly.

"Am I your fucking secretary?" Kita huffed out a breath.

"Can you input the names into the people search program you use?" Dwayne smiled. "My handwriting is terrible."

They wanted her to record the names. Fine.

She opened a new tab and prepared to take notes on the judge's life. "Give me name, spelling, how you're associated with them, and what they do."

First the judge rattled off his assistant's name, Vanessa. That settled why she was pissed that Kita went the fundraiser with the judge. "She's my assistant, and ah, she handles the office correspondence and puts out any fires while I'm in court."

"Relationship?" Alex bulleted out.

"Our relationship is…also sexual in nature."

"Judge, just give us the details. Pussyfooting around the topic is just going to make for awkward questions." Kita cut to the chase, annoyed at the way he hesitated.

"Fine. Yes." He rubbed at a particularly deep scar in the wood table. "She has been my mistress for the past six months."

Kita nodded. "Next."

He reluctantly mentioned the bailiff and their sexual relationship. Also in the past six months. "Concurrently?" Alex asked what she hadn't had a chance to wrap her mind around.

"Yes."

He continued on, naming his masseuse and his tennis pro. Jesus, four women. And he was having sex with all of them. "Are they aware that your…liaisons were not exclusive?"

The judge stiffened as if Kita had impugned his honor. "Of course."

"Is that everyone?" Alex asked the question everyone wondered about.

"Ah, not quite." The judge cleared his throat. "Darla Nichols."

"The congresswoman?" Kita blurted out.

"Yes, dear."

Huh. That could make for some difficult and uncomfortable encounters. The silence went on. "Anyone else?"

Now the judge appeared discomfited. He didn't speak.

"Judge?" Alex prodded.

"Colleen Adams."

Wait, what? He'd had sex with Marsh's mother? Her somewhat adoptive mother? The one he was divorced from and had been since Marsh was little? Of course the reason for the divorce was completely obvious after the past fifteen minutes.

Kita waited.

"We have sexual relations once a month."

Kita was trying to come to grips with that information. He'd practically blown her mind. She thought Colleen Adams hated her ex-husband's guts just like her son did. Maybe it was some sort of love/hate relationship. Or…she couldn't even fathom. She had nothing.

"Anyone else?" There was nothing in Alex's words or face that betrayed his agitation but Kita sensed the underlying disgust that permeated his opinion of the judge.

"Ah, there is one last person."

More?

The silence bore down on them while the judge looked at Kita. Something in his face gave away his discomfort and the fact that he thought it would matter to her. She wasn't going to like whoever he named next. But she literally had no idea who it might be.

"Joyce Nguyen."

Kita sat frozen. She hadn't typed the name in her spreadsheet. She hadn't moved, hadn't breathed.

Everyone in the room stilled. Alex was staring at the judge with a puzzled look on his face. "And is the relationship sexual in nature?"

Kita held her breath. Her heart beat with frenzy in her throat, so hard she could barely breathe.

"Yes."

The judge was having sex with her mother?

Holy shit.

Chapter 14

The mood in the room had shifted wildly but Alex had no idea why.

Kita's expressive eyes had widened and she hadn't blinked. The judge on the other hand had shifted his gaze as if he was trying to look anywhere but at Alex's tough partner.

And when had he started thinking of Kita as his? Because that thought was beyond possessive.

What was he missing?

The judge finally said, "I figured out why you look familiar." Was there a tinge of red on his face?

Now that Alex thought about it, his attitude toward Kita had been more reserved this morning. The slightly leering looks were gone. So Joyce Nguyen must be related to Kita.

"Your mother?" Shep wondered.

Alex wanted to cuff him upside the head. Dwayne gave Kita a sympathetic look.

"Moving on." Kita's deer-in-the-headlights expression had hardened. "We need to run checks on all these women."

"All of them?" the judge blustered.

"Someone, a woman, is making threats against your person," Kita clipped out. "Not only that, they have managed to get extremely close to you while you were under protection. By all appearances they seem to be extremely pissed off."

Jesus, no wonder. He was practically fucking half of Washington.

Kita tapped away at her computer, entering the details they had into some sort of search database.

She hesitated for a second, and he figured she was about to enter her mother's info.

Kita's face was completely blank, but he could sense her distress, as if he was attuned to her in a way that transcended mere physical connection. He wanted to take care of her. To comfort her. But she'd like that about as much as she liked the judge sleeping with her mother. He shifted the conversation, giving her time to get her shit together. "Any defendants who were unhappy with rulings in your court?"

"Son, for every case in my court there's always one party unhappy with the outcome."

Except that in most of his cases, one of the parties was the US government. Alex doubted the government was threatening the judge.

"Anyone particularly disgruntled or a contentious case recently?" While the judge contemplated his options, Alex headed for the kitchen counter and poured himself a cup of coffee. The small kitchen was stocked with paper plates, plastic forks and knives, and Styrofoam cups. He pulled down another Styrofoam cup from the kitchen cabinet, pressed the hot water dispenser, and dropped in a teabag for his partner.

Courtesy. That's all it was.

But because he tried to be honest with himself, he acknowledged the need to take care of her. Even in a little way. He added one sweetener and one creamer and stirred, then set it in front of Kita. He wanted to put his hand on her shoulder, give her a squeeze for support, but that would go over as well as the judge's confession.

Judge Adams tapped a long finger against his mouth. "There are several cases that come to mind, but all the defendants are in federal prison right now."

Dwayne pressed the judge. "What about family members? Or business partners?"

Good thoughts. Because clearly their perpetrator wasn't in prison. Just like poor Mr. Gauss from yesterday.

"Gauss was the only family member who threatened me."

But Alex's attention was fractured. He was listening to the judge and wondering how Kita was handling the revelation about her mother. Except maybe beyond the surprise factor she didn't care. He couldn't get a read on her and that bugged him.

He liked to understand his partners, liked to understand what made them tick, so he could predict their actions and accommodate for their responses to a case and its stimuli.

But so far Kita Kim wasn't conforming to any of his preconceived expectations.

Shep was giving him a funny look and Alex realized he was staring at Kita's delicate hand, her fingers curled around the throwaway cup, her unpainted nails neatly trimmed.

A knock at the front door galvanized everyone into action.

Immediately all three agents had their weapons out. Except for Kita, whose weapon was in the purse in the bag the other agents had just brought back. But she was on alert.

Alex ordered her, "Take the judge in the back bedroom and wait for the all clear."

Kita's eyes sparked, outraged. "Why me?"

"Because you're the only one who isn't armed." Alex didn't want her in the first line of fire, but she was his partner and he needed to let go of his worry about it. He respected her abilities. "And I know you have mad hand-to-hand skills but you don't have a weapon."

"Good save," Dwayne said under his breath.

"Except if the judge becomes incapacitated, I can't carry him." She made a valid point.

"Fine. Dwayne, you get the judge to the first bedroom."

Dwayne escorted the judge down the hallway, and once they were in the room with the door closed, Alex gestured to the front door.

Shep and Alex took up positions on either side of the frame. Who the hell was at the door? "How the fuck do people keep finding him?"

Alex gestured to Kita to stand behind the half wall that separated the living room and dining room and was not in a clear line of sight to the front door. If the person on the other side started shooting, the odds they would hit her were slim.

It sucked, but he wanted to protect her any way he could.

She hesitated, as if she were going to argue, then took position.

The living room sported a couple of folding chairs. Only the television appeared to have been manufactured in this century. The state-of-the-art surveillance system connected to the television displayed four quadrants of pictures. The front door. The garage. The back door and the basement exit.

Whoever was at the front door was standing too close to the door and out of camera range. All the security cameras caught was a wool coat on a woman's back, but nothing else was detectable on the screen. The person's shadow was visible behind the glass and curtains that covered the windowed panels on either side of the single door. Alex frowned. Not very security minded. They had to know that there were agents inside.

Right?

Alex crouched behind the other half wall with a direct line of sight to the front door and the security monitor mounted at the ceiling.

The knock came again.

What assassin or stalker in their right mind knocked? Maybe this was something else?

"Hello?" A female voice called from the porch. Suddenly she moved and tried to peer into the living room, her hands cupped around her eyes and pressed to the glass.

Vanessa, the judge's assistant.

Alex relaxed slightly. Shep too. But Kita stayed on guard. "Women are just as dangerous as men."

Truth.

Protocol dictated that they get the judge out. The safe house had been compromised.

"Before we move again," Kita whispered, "let's talk to the judge."

She sprinted down the hallway and opened the bedroom door. Shit. That wasn't protocol. "I think I know where she's going with this," Shep murmured.

"Doesn't matter." Alex's blood pressure rose as he heard her yelling at the judge. Also against protocol. After a minute, Kita, Dwayne and the judge reentered the living room. Dwayne glanced between him and Kita, a knowing look in his gaze.

Shit. Alex hadn't even considered that Dwayne would figure out something had happened between them.

It wasn't technically against the rules, but their behavior had skated a fine line.

Alex could feel the flush creep over his face.

Shep's attention sharpened. "What?"

"Nothing," Alex muttered. He should never have touched her.

"Bobby here told his assistant where we were."

"Are you kidding me?" Alex rounded on the judge. "She's on the list."

"But if we don't answer, she'll be persistent." Kita argued. "We need to let her in before the whole freaking neighborhood knows he's here."

Within a few seconds, they had the judge secured again, and Kita headed for the door.

She opened the front door cautiously.

"You," the assistant accused. She burst inside the house, and the front door banged shut. "Are you holding the judge against his will?"

In a lightning-fast move, Kita slammed her up against the wall, one arm twisted high along her back, her fingers pressed between her shoulder blades. Her oversized striped tote bag fell to the floor with a thud.

The assistant yelped. "What are you doing? You stupid whore."

The insult rolled off Kita's back. "My job."

"I'm going to press charges against you, freaking lunatic," the woman hissed. Meanwhile the judge had come out of the kitchen and Alex wanted to punch the lascivious smirk off his face.

"Dear Lord, it's a catfight," the judge murmured.

Alex saw red.

The slow boil that had been simmering all morning erupted. Frustration at his reluctant, rule-breaking partner, irritation with the judge, who Alex was convinced still wasn't telling them the whole truth, and the situation in general, which pushed all his protocol-following buttons.

His anger erupted into a threat. "Judge. I'm going to give you one minute to explain yourself, and if I'm not satisfied with the answer, I'm going to change your protective custody to a mandatory confinement to a federal facility in order to keep you safe."

The judge started to bluster again. "Why, I never."

The assistant was attempting to struggle against Kita's hold but his rebel was having none of that. She'd put her foot between the secretary's feet and grabbed the woman's hair, putting her in a headlock. The woman squealed.

Kita barked, "Shut up."

"Now, Judge." Alex loomed over the older man.

"Fine. I had some work to do so I gave Vanessa the address so she could drop off my papers. I'm a very busy man," he replied pompously.

Alex reined in his temper, but it was extremely difficult. "You realize we're trying to keep you safe." And he hadn't succeeded too well, since he was at a near shout when he finished the sentence.

Shep was eyeing Alex like he'd never seen him before. At least this side of him. Alex had to get under control.

"Hey, Judge," Kita said pleasantly.

"Yes, darlin'."

"You could well be a very un-busy *dead* man if you keep announcing your secret locations to people."

At that the assistant shut up. "What's she talking about, Bobby?"

"The judge's threatening letters have escalated to personal attacks." Kita turned Vanessa to face the agents. "You know anything about that?"

"Attacks?" Her voice rose convincingly, but she wouldn't be the first woman scorned to lie. "Oh my God, are you okay?"

The judge smiled, baring his white teeth. "I'm fine, darlin'."

Alex wanted to gag. Did women really fall for his bullshit?

"What are we going to do about her?" Kita's hold hadn't relaxed on the petite redhead; if anything she'd ratcheted Vanessa's arms up higher behind her back.

The judge took a step toward the pair of women. "Quit manhandling my assistant."

"All due respect, *sir*," Kita said insolently. "I don't work for you. I work for him." She jerked her head toward Alex.

While he appreciated her support, they didn't need to piss off the judge any more than Alex already had.

Alex pulled out his cell. "We'll have to get someone here to take her to the local office for questioning."

Vanessa whimpered. "But I was just doing my job."

Alex picked up the woman's tote bag and riffled through the contents, which consisted of mostly makeup—dear God, how many lipsticks did one woman need?—a wallet with a thousand dollars in cash, pens, a notebook, a single manila envelope, and several condom packets.

Alex raised his brows. Had the judge really been hoping for a little afternoon delight?

Something was off about this whole thing. Judge Adams wasn't stupid. He might be a sex addict but he had to have an extremely bright mind. "What did you have her bring?"

"Just trial papers." Judge Adams flicked his hand dismissing the question.

But Alex's instincts were clamoring.

"What did he have you bring?" Alex got right up in the woman's personal space.

The woman tilted her head back, eyes closed, lips trembling. Was she trying to play him?

"He got another note."

"Why didn't you notify the US Marshals?" Kita asked before he could. "That's protocol."

"Because Bobby wanted to see it first."

Alex fought the urge to curse, long and loud.

"We can't protect you if we don't know where the threat is coming from." Kita spoke to the judge. "The protocol exists for a reason."

Wait, in what bizarre world did Kita quote the rules? Alex peered at her, as if he could discern from staring into her black gaze what the hell she was thinking.

She smirked at him, her lips curved so that a small nearly unnoticeable dimple appeared next to her nose.

"Why don't we all take it down a notch?" Shep was the voice of reason.

Within a few minutes, they were seated at the scarred table. Dwayne and Shep perched on the deep windowsills while Kita, Alex, the judge and Vanessa huddled at the table.

"Show us." Kita turned the laptop so that the redhead could pull up the email. Instead, she reached in her oversized tote bag.

All the agents tensed.

Alex sat straighter in his chair. "A physical note?"

"Yes. It was on my desk when I got in this morning."
Her fingers trembled as she tried to smooth down her hair.
Her long red nails caught his attention.

"Did you touch it?"

"Ah, yes." She flushed. "But as soon as I figured out
what it was, I slipped it in the manila envelope."

They needed sterile gloves and an evidence bag. He had
a feeling that the paper was going to match the generic 20-lb
paper of the letter with the fake anthrax.

"What's it say?"

"'Your child will pay. Trouble never comes alone.'"

Your child. Did the judge have another kid they were
unaware of?

"They threatened Marsh?"

It was the first time Alex had seen the judge rattled. His
face whitened, and within seconds he looked every one of
his sixty-odd years.

But what caught Alex's attention was the look on Kita's
face. There wasn't any. She was stoic, her eyes flat and
vacant.

"What do you know about this?" Alex accused her. Was
this why the judge wanted Adams-Larsen in on this
protection detail from the beginning?

"I don't know what you mean." Kita blinked.

"This is not the time for evasiveness," he growled.

"You think I know what 'trouble never comes alone'
means?" Kita threw up her hands. "It could be anything.
Maybe there's more than one perpetrator. Maybe there's
more than one attack. Maybe it pertains to more than one
situation. How the hell should I know?"

"Don't hold out on me," Alex warned.

Dwayne was watching the byplay between the two of
them like a ping-pong match. But the blank look on his face

and the little crinkles fanning out from his eyes convinced Alex that he had no idea what was going on either.

Alex shoved his chair away from the table, and the loud screech rent the air. "Can I speak to you alone?"

Kita raised a brow. "Protocol dictates that we share information with all the marshals in charge."

"You really going to quote rules at me right now, Kita?"

"Fine." She strode sullenly into the first bedroom.

Alex shut the door with a snap. "What is going on?"

"The judge is an idiot and Barbie isn't far behind." Beneath the flippant exterior something was wrong.

What he wanted to say was, "Talk to me." But what came out of his mouth was far more stilted. "I can't condone your spot on this team if you aren't going to share intelligence with me." And of course, that was going to piss her off. He knew that but it was as if he were watching them above their bodies, and he could see the train wreck coming.

"Are you seriously threatening to kick me off this team?" She propped her fists on her hips and stepped right into his space. She jabbed her finger into his breastbone. "You have no precedent."

He stepped into her. His chest bumped her confined breasts. "You're keeping information that might be tangential or even crucial to this case. Tell me what you know or I'll file an official report about your conduct." Why had he bought in to her vulnerability? She was purposely hamstringing their investigation and case. He should have never agreed to subvert the regular process.

Kita didn't back down. But finally she blew out a breath. "I don't know if it's related, but…."

"What, Kita?"

"I'm breaking a damn confidence here, back the fuck off."

Alex waited.

"Marsh isn't on a special assignment."

The judge's son?

"Where is he then?"

"That would be the question, wouldn't it?"

"So you're saying he's missing?"

"Not exactly missing," she hedged.

"Exactly what then?"

"He told Jill he was going to take some time off." Kita looked him in the eyes. This close they were nearly eye level, and their mouths were aligned perfectly.

Alex waited.

"But it's been over a month and she hasn't seen him."

Kita rubbed the back of her neck. "And before you ask, he does do this sometimes, except he's never been incommunicado for this length of time."

Alex considered the information. "So it's possible the letter writer is trying to draw him out."

"It would appear that way."

"We need to interview all the women on that list." Alex rubbed his thumb over the bare skin of her biceps absently, thinking through their priorities.

"Why women?"

"This feels very personal."

"True, but what if the women have significant others?"

Alex sighed. "Hopefully the team going through the court records will find something. But my gut says that this isn't about a federal court case, it's far more intimate than that."

Kita's eyes sparkled, her earlier annoyance had disappeared, and the band around his chest loosened, allowing him to breathe. He didn't like to be at cross purposes with her.

"Your gut?"

He smiled wryly. "Everyone has instincts."

Her cheeks curved in amusement, her face light, almost happy. "Yes, but I'm surprised Mr. Rule Follower is listening."

Chapter 15

Alex drove through the crowded streets of DC with Kita by his side. He wasn't even sure how it happened, but Dwayne and Shep had stayed with the judge, going over his recent court cases, combing through the transcripts looking for any threatening language, while he and Kita went on the suspect interviews.

They'd had the Marshals come get Vanessa. They were guarding her and going through her records to confirm that she hadn't had outside contact with a third party. Alex was pretty sure she was harmless and innocent, but never underestimate the rage of a woman with a grudge.

They had already tackled the masseuse and the tennis pro at the same club.

Both women only had positive things to say about the judge. They knew he was sleeping with more than one woman and were fine with it. The only time they'd been upset was when they found out he was receiving threats. Even then, their main concern was the judge's safety.

That had been eye-opening. Apparently Judge Adams

had a certain amount of…stamina for an older man. Both women had been thrilled to expound on his attributes.

"I may need to bleach my eyes and ears," Kita muttered.

He figured she was goofing around, trying to keep her mind off the next interviews. "I'll take your mother—"

"Joyce Nguyen," she said flatly. "She is not honorable enough for that title."

"Okay." Alex blew out his breath. "You take Marsh's mom while I interview Nguyen. Try and see if you can get a line on where Marsh is. It's possible that he's in danger too."

"Marsh can take care of himself." The affection in her voice irritated him. Marsh, the wonderful. If he was so wonderful, where the hell was he?

"What's Colleen Adams like?"

"I can't believe…."

Alex knew what she was inferring. The judge's relationship with Colleen Adams boggled the mind. "How long have they been divorced?"

"Since Marsh was ten or so."

"Over twenty years." And yet they still had sex once a month. Alex raised his eyebrows.

Kita shuddered. "I don't want to think about it."

Alex drove through a residential neighborhood in the heart of Georgetown. The gracious old mansions were set back from the street. Decorative iron gates sent a clear message, "Keep Out," and if you were stupid enough to ignore that, the posted security company placards on the lawn near the front steps were a more modern version of "Don't Come Knocking."

Kita and Marsh had literally lived next door to each other.

On the sidewalk they split, Alex going left, Kita going right. He started to remind her, "Remember—"

"Got it, Rule Boy."

Alex huffed out a breath. "See you in a few."

He headed toward the enormous craftsman style house. The garden beyond the gate overflowed with water features and lush green tropical plants. The mini-Zen garden near the porch was a surprise too. The peaceful atmosphere was at odds with the intel he had regarding Mrs. Nguyen.

He glanced around the carefully maintained oasis and then vaulted up the stairs and knocked on the door. After a significant pause, the door opened to reveal a tiny Asian woman. "Come in, Deputy Marshal Saunders." She'd lost most of her accent but hints remained in slightly dropped Rs. "Let's keep this interview to a minimum."

He could see hints of Kita in the shape of Mrs. Nguyen's eyes and the keen intelligence that lingered in her stare. But her demeanor was cold, even judgmental.

"Answer my questions honestly and we should be done fairly quickly."

"She didn't want to come in," she sneered.

So she had been watching. Odd. Because Alex hadn't mentioned Kita.

"If you're referring to Ms. Kim—"

"Bah," she hissed.

Alex watched her closely. "She is conducting a separate interview."

Joyce Nguyen's eyes widened. "This is about Bobby?"

He was pleased she didn't pretend an ignorance. "Yes."

Alex glanced around curiously. So this was where Kita grew up? While the exterior was peaceful and tranquil, the interior was sparse. The bare wood floors had tatami mats. Ornate rosewood sofas carved with ancient symbols were grouped around a low coffee table. Bold red silk cushions had scattered pillows with some birds on them.

An earthenware tea pot with an iron handle rested on a rectangular serving platter. Steam gently swirled in the air.

"Be seated."

Alex sat on the hard cushion of the couch. He pulled out a small recorder. "If you agree, I'd like to tape our conversation."

Her hand like a blade, she made a sharp cutting motion. "Makes no difference."

"State your name and occupation."

They went through the standard identifying questions with Joyce Nguyen responding as minimally as possible. But Alex didn't get the sense she was trying to be obstructionist. She just didn't like to waste words.

Joyce Nguyen. Professor of Graduate Asian Studies for a small liberal arts university. Sixty years old. She was first generation American of Vietnamese and Chinese descent. She had retaken her maiden name when her husband died. Kita's father had been Vietnamese and Scottish of all things.

"How do you know Judge Adams?"

"Neighbor."

She poured a single cup of tea. Her stare was defiant as she sipped. Alex raised his eyebrows.

"And how long have you and Mr. Adams been engaged in sexual relations?"

"None of your business."

"How long has your affair been active?"

Her face flat, she stared him down, refusing to answer.

"Ms. Nguyen, perhaps you're unaware but this is a federal investigation regarding threats made against the judge."

For the first time, she showed some emotion. "Is Bobby

okay?" She leaned forward in her seat, her tea steaming and unforgotten.

"There have been several attempts, which the US Marshals were able to stop with the help of Kita."

"Is Bobby okay?"

"Your daughter was injured in the first attempt." Alex's temper boiled over. "Does that matter at all?"

"I don't see how that information is relative to your questions."

Alex had to forcibly rein in his anger. "You are correct." Thank God Kita had gotten away from this cold, cold woman. "The judge is fine. For now."

Her relief was visible.

"Do you have any reason to harm him?"

"Of course not."

"And are you aware of anyone who might wish him harm?"

"Everyone loves Bobby."

Alex resisted the real urge to put his fist through the decorative shoji screen. He pulled out his business card and handed it to the woman, trying hard not to let their fingers brush.

"If you think of anything that could help our investigation, please don't hesitate to call me."

"Show yourself out."

Alex hesitated, wanting to defend Kita, wanting to berate this cold woman about her treatment of a young girl.

Instead, he hustled out of the dark house, wonder swirling in his gut. How had Kita turned out so normal? So warm? So full of light?

KITA ASCENDED the steps to Marsh's childhood home. A soft smile of remembrance curved her lips at the carved pumpkins lining the steps, the hay bales on the porch, along with a stuffed scarecrow and bundles of cornstalks.

One of the many things she loved about Colleen Adams's house was the sense of warmth and welcome that wrapped around her like a big warm wool sweater. Before she could ring the bell, the front door flung open.

"Kita!" Colleen Adams enveloped her in a hug and squeezed tightly. "I've missed you, honey."

She was surrounded in a cloud of White Linen perfume, instantly winging her back to that horrible night in the hospital. The cold, the lights, the noise, and then Colleen and Marsh had come and saved her.

Kita knew those hours had shaped her. She longed to be able to do that, to be that person for someone else. She wasn't warm like Mrs. Adams but she burned with the desire to give someone else the gift of safety she'd been given.

Colleen curled her arm around Kita's shoulders and practically dragged her inside. "I want to hear all about how things are going. You haven't been by for Sunday dinner in at least a month."

Remorse nagged at Kita. "Sorry, I've been working at this shelter and— "

"Honey, I didn't say that to make you feel guilty." Her voice softened and she patted Kita's shoulder. "I just miss catching up with you—and Marsh."

Marsh. She was going to have to see if Colleen had any information about her son. But first, she had to focus on the situation regarding the judge.

Kita followed her surrogate mother into the kitchen. The rest of the house was more formal, more stuffy with antiques and fancy rugs and family portraits, but the hub of the home was Colleen Adams's kitchen. Warm, butter-yellow walls and brilliant white trim framed the room. A spacious island with amber hanging lights and smooth granite countertops was where she and Marsh had eaten breakfast years ago.

The kitchen table was one of those old farm tables with spindled legs and a honey gold finish. An amber glass bowl with gourds and mini pumpkins sat in the middle of the table, and the calendar beside the phone was turned to October, depicting a goofy cat with a knitted pumpkin stalk cap on its head.

"You want some tea?"

"Sure." Kita headed toward the ancient Aga range. "But I can get it."

"Nonsense." Colleen tied an apron at her waist and bustled around, setting up the kettle and a little ceramic plate with sesame tea cookies, Kita's favorite. "Let me spoil you a bit."

A happy warmth settled over Kita as they chatted about everyday things. Colleen's garden association, her weekly coffee with a group of DC's movers and shakers, and the upcoming election.

Kita dreaded bringing this up, not wanting to cause her honorary mother any distress, but she had to ask. There must be some horrible reason that the judge made Colleen engage with him on a monthly basis.

Her stomach curdled at the thought of upsetting Colleen.

"You going to tell me why you're here in the middle of a workday?"

Kita flushed. "I, ah, need to ask you a question about the judge." This was harder than she thought.

Colleen sighed heavily, but she met Kita's gaze head-on. Her lips curved in a bittersweet smile but there was no apology on her face or in her voice. "My relationship with Bobby is…complicated."

Colleen had kicked the judge out years ago. Kita didn't understand. But she kept silent.

"He is not a man for commitment."

Kita snorted. She slapped her fingers over her mouth. "Sorry."

Colleen's laugh was like a pretty tinkling waterfall. "I am well aware of my ex-husband's faults. But he is a generous and absolutely gifted lover." She threaded her spindly fingers together, and her hands seemed more fragile than Kita remembered.

Now Colleen flushed. Her gently lined face turned a deep red. "And so once a month, we have an assignation. At the Hay-Adams. It's romantic and lovely and there are no expectations on either side."

Colleen was clearly at peace with her choices. So who was Kita to judge her? But with a self-aware clarity, she realized that she wasn't cut out for that kind of relationship. "Um, okay." But her lack of understanding must have come through.

"Oh, honey." Colleen brushed a hand over Kita's shoulder as if touching her could impart the reasons why she had sex with her cheating ex on a regular basis. "Perhaps one day you'll understand, but I certainly hope not."

Kita's throat tightened.

"Can I ask why this subject came up?"

Kita's world had literally tilted on its axis in the past few minutes so she blurted out the cause for her visit. "Well the judge is receiving threats, so we're—"

"Is Bobby okay?" Colleen's bony fingers gripped Kita's wrist like a boa constrictor squeezing prey. Her voice had risen and her whole body quivered with worry.

"He's fine." Kita patted Colleen's fingers. "We're taking good care of him. But we're looking for anyone who might have a grudge against him."

"And you're checking out all the women he...."

Now Kita really flushed. "Yes."

Thankfully, at that moment, the doorbell chimed.

"I'll get it." Kita said, "I should probably get going any way."

But Colleen followed close behind her. Kita peered through the security peephole. Alex.

"It's my partner." Kita opened the door.

"How you doing?" he asked before she could get a word out. There was something in his voice. The concern on his face was for her. He seemed to be one step away from grabbing her.

Kita blinked. So much emotion vibrated in the simple question. "Fine." She turned and introduced the two of them.

Colleen shook Alex's hand, a melancholy smile on her face. "Well." She sighed.

"What's wrong?"

"I'd always hoped that one day...you and Marsh." She fluttered her hand in front of her face. "Well, that's a good nevermind now."

Colleen glanced between her and Alex.

What? "Oh, we're just—"

"I see exactly what you are." Colleen squeezed Kita in a great big tight warm hug. Her arms still represented that haven of security and protection.

Then Colleen grabbed up Alex in a hug. "You take care of my girl now."

"Yes, ma'am." Alex's brow crinkled in a clearly puzzled expression.

Colleen stepped back, ran her gaze over Alex one more time. Then she nodded. "When you and Marsh come for Sunday dinner, bring your friend."

Perfect. Colleen Adams had given her the perfect segue into asking about Marsh without drawing any undue attention.

"Have you talked to him lately?" Kita asked, not wanting to alarm his mother but her worry continued to grow.

"Not in a few weeks." Colleen gave her a puzzled look. "Haven't you?"

"Ah, we've been on conflicting assignments for the last month. I've barely seen him." As in not at all.

"You and your secret projects." Colleen nipped the deadhead off a bright yellow mum.

Beside her Alex stiffened.

She clutched the browned petals in a gentle fist. "Keep the judge safe, honey."

"We will."

"Love you."

That awkward moment happened every time Colleen Adams expressed her feelings. And feeling like she was still that seventeen-year-old abuse victim with a broken wrist and battered face, Kita ducked at the outright show of affection. "Ah, love you too."

Chapter 16

The car ride to their last interview was silent. Alex had too many thoughts running through his brain after their interviews.

"Last on the list," Kita finally said.

"We should probably compare notes on our interviews." Shit, he'd like to forget his conversation with her mother.

"Sure." She shifted in the front seat of the government-issued sedan.

"Thoughts on Colleen Adams."

"Not a suspect," Kita clipped out, no hesitation. "What about Joyce Nguyen?"

"Not a suspect either." Alex hesitated.

"Spit it out."

"The only time she showed any emotion was when she found out the judge was in danger." He wanted to apologize for her mother. He wanted to go back and give her a piece of his mind. To take her to task for clearly not caring about her daughter. She had known Kita was at the Adams's house but she hadn't asked about her at all. Hadn't even blinked when he'd told her Kita had been injured.

Joyce Nguyen's frigid attitude nearly gave him frostbite.

When they'd pulled away from the curb after the interviews, Alex had noted Kita's lingering look at her childhood home. She'd returned Colleen Adams's affection awkwardly, but her final act had been one inscrutable glance at her mother's garden.

He burned with the need to touch Kita, to soothe her. Except it was really about soothing himself. Her mother's defiance and indifference touched off a foreign emotion. The desire to shield her from motherly rejection was strong. Except he knew what she'd say. She could take care of herself. And he knew that, he did, but he couldn't help but wish that she would let him in.

Kita rubbed her wrist. "Same with Colleen."

Alex couldn't help but be surprised. The guy certainly maintained a loyal stable of sexual conquests. "So the randy old judge apparently inspires devotion in women. A staggering amount." Conversely, he'd been a pain in Alex's ass from the moment they'd met.

"Yeah. Weird."

He'd seen the clear affection between Marsh Adams's mother and Kita. "You sure you're objective enough?" They couldn't afford to overlook a potential suspect because she had an emotional connection to one of the suspects.

"Colleen Adams taught me everything about self-acceptance and being strong. She taught me to stick up for myself. To defend myself. She gave me the tools to become the person I am today, so fuck you very much. She has more integrity in her pinky than most people have in their entire body. And she would never, ever harm someone, including, it turns out, her ex-husband."

And there was the fighting spirit that irritated him and intrigued him at the same time. "Fair enough."

"And another thing, wait…what?"

"I just wanted to make sure you weren't compromised."

"Seriously?" She twisted in her seat, her face a mask of annoyance.

"I trust your judgement."

All her gruff anger disintegrated. "Okay. Ah, thank you."

Alex grinned. "I feel like you aren't typically at a loss for words."

"Yeah, no." She smiled sheepishly. "Not usually. By the way, sorry about the weirdness at the end. She wants to see me happy."

Alex was pleased she had someone looking out for her. Especially since her biological mother was a complete bitch.

However, he definitely didn't want to discuss Colleen Adams's not-so-veiled references to them. As if she had some sort of couple-sniffing radar and knew they had slept together.

He liked Kita. Yeah, the sex had been smoking hot. But they were totally wrong for each other. Even if in bed they communicated on a completely different plane.

"It's all good." He stopped before the conversation could get more awkward. But he did wonder, "What's the deal with you and Marsh Adams?"

"Friends," she said quickly.

"That's it?" He didn't know why he didn't let it go but the urge to press her didn't fade.

"He's like my older brother." Kita didn't fidget. Her hands rested casually in her lap. "Surely you can understand that."

Alex cleared his throat. "Yeah."

"He looks out for me."

Alex felt the pang of regret all the way to his toes. He

hadn't looked out for his brother. And that decision had shaped their lives. While he'd become a rule-follower, Andrew was the daredevil.

It turned out Drew had liked the rush even at nine years old. He'd never outgrown it. These days he was in the Rangers. Half the time Alex didn't even know where in the world Drew was, and the other half he catalogued new scars and injuries and hoped his brother didn't get himself killed. Being less than a year apart, you would think they'd be closer. Their mother blamed Alex, and he blamed himself too.

For every crazy thing his brother had done, Alex tried to compensate by being even more straitlaced. Which didn't work. But he tried. Drew prodded Alex to let go more often and Alex cautioned his brother to think before he jumped.

Their relationship had never been the same since the accident.

"Where'd you go?" Kita tilted her head at him.

The last thing he wanted to do was explain his mixed emotions about his brother. "Let's go see the honorable Ms. Nichols."

They had called the congresswoman's office and she'd agreed to fit them into her busy schedule. Her staff's attitude had been borderline antagonistic, one assumed because neither Kita nor Alex were her constituents and they had no political pull for her upcoming campaign. Since she was cooperating, minimally, he'd leave it alone for now. But if she stonewalled them, Alex could make things difficult for her. Just because she served in the House of Representatives didn't mean that she was exempt from answering their questions.

They were meeting at a diner a few blocks away from the Sofitel on 15th. The congresswoman was attending a luncheon at the hotel. She blocked out twenty minutes of her time. She'd suggested the diner, away from the hotel dining room and Le Bar, which was still considered a meeting place for DC's influential and influenced. He guessed she didn't want to be seen with them. Explaining that she had to answer questions from federal marshals likely wasn't high on the list of qualities her donors were interested in sponsoring.

They settled into a booth in the corner. Alex faced the door and Kita sat across from him, her back to the entrance. The vinyl seats and Formica tabletops were throwbacks to an earlier era. A neon sign in the window flashed "Open" in bright red, and the daily specials were written on a chalkboard. An old-fashioned cash register sat at the end of the counter near the row of swivel stools.

While they waited, Alex ordered a coffee, Kita an iced tea. The silence around them was comfortable, easy. He hated having to interrogate Darla Nichols. He couldn't imagine that a sitting member of the House of Representatives was involved in stalking a federal judge but she was on the list of lovers. And that meant she had to be questioned.

Congresswoman Nichols made her way to their table. She had on the DC power suit, navy with a tight skirt, white blouse, demurely cut, and a buttoned blazer. Her official House of Representatives pin with the eagle and the seal on her lapel was her only adornment besides the plain gold wedding band on her left ring finger. She wore matching navy pumps in a low chunky heel and bold red lipstick.

Alex stood as she approached the table. Kita turned around, and if he hadn't been observing Darla Nichols closely he would have missed her slight falter when she recognized his partner.

"Deputy Marshal Saunders, I presume?" The congresswoman ignored Kita. "What's the judge's aide doing here?"

"Ms. Kim is working with us on the judge's case." Alex didn't mention Adams-Larsen or the fact that Kita wasn't really the judge's aide.

He hadn't given her office any information except that he was investigating a threat to a client, and her name had come up and he wanted to know if she knew anything. She didn't react but slid gracefully into the seat next to Kita and across from Alex. She arched a dark eyebrow. "Bobby is the case?"

Alex inclined his head.

"Well, I've only got fifteen minutes, so let's get to it." She smiled, politely but with a subtle edge that implied she'd be willing to be more than polite if the interest was there.

Her obvious ploy to distract him was annoying. But Alex remained professional. Before he could continue, Kita said tightly, "Your name came up during an investigation regarding threats against Judge Adams." Her words held a combativeness that no one could miss.

Shit. This was not the time to antagonize a sitting congresswoman.

Alex's blood pressure rose. If Darla Nichols took offense, they'd have a whole different problem on their hands.

Darla swiveled to face Kita. "Why would I threaten Bobby? He's an influential man with the ear of people who have the ability to place me on the committees I want, aiding in my career advancement." She shook her head, implying "silly girl," and turned back toward Alex.

Thank God, she hadn't taken offense at Kita's hostile attitude. They couldn't just go around accusing a distinguished congresswoman of stalking.

His worry blew away when she smiled at him again. This time he smiled back.

"Let's make this quick, shall we?" Darla said crisply. "Yes. I have had sexual relations with Judge Adams. Yes, I know that he is actively involved with several women. No, I'm not jealous. Bobby and I have an understanding. He's been influential in helping me meet the right people in DC."

So cold. Delivered with no emotion beyond a jaded amusement and clear boredom, as if they were wasting her time with this line of questioning.

"So you are unaware of the threats to his person?" Alex asked before Kita could piss her off again.

"Eh. People say they milk chickens."

Kita frowned. "I've never heard that saying before."

"My grandmother, who raised me, was from the USSR," Darla said smoothly. "It was one of her most favorite sayings. It means 'don't believe all the rumors.'"

Russian heritage. Interesting.

But the threats to the judge were more than just rumors.

"Anything else?" Darla Nichols glanced at her tank watch, clearly dismissing them.

Alex figured it couldn't hurt to ask for her opinion. "Do you have any ideas why someone would be targeting the judge?"

Darla jerked her head toward Kita. "Maybe you should be looking at his staff."

"Bobby knows I wouldn't threaten him." Basically implying that they were close. Very close.

"Let me give you a little advice, chickie." Her low voice sliced through the clinking of cups and utensils, the ebb and swell of murmured conversations. "Use Bobby. But be aware that the only person he cares about his himself, and his son."

There'd been a note in Darla's voice, just for a moment, that tripped Alex's switch.

Kita raised an eyebrow. "You know Marsh?"

The animosity between the two women nearly drowned Alex. Just like when his brother was caught in that rushing stream, he couldn't save anyone from the coming disaster.

"Of him." Darla slid out of the booth and stood. "The judge is extremely proud of him."

Kita snorted. "Well, let me tell you, the admiration is not mutual."

"Really?" The change in Darla was subtle. Her contemptuous gaze raked Kita up and down. "And how would a mere aide know that?"

Kita's eyes sparkled with temper. "We've been best friends since middle school, b—"

"And I think we're done here." Alex put his hand over Darla's clenched fists.

Fortunately, Kita had pulled back and not actually called the congresswoman a bitch but it was a damn close call.

"Congresswoman, thank you so much for your time." Alex tried to smooth over the tension.

"Please don't call me again," she said. "I am not interested in the judge except as a means to an end. Which could not be accomplished if he were dead and I couldn't carry on my dear husband's legacy."

"Of course." Alex hoped they hadn't completely burned her as a witness. "Thank you for your time."

Darla glanced once more at her watch. "I'm late." She shot Kita one more speculative look, then strode out of the diner as if she owned the damn place.

Once she was gone, Alex rounded on his partner. "What the hell?"

"She pissed me off," she said defiantly.

"And so you just decided to insult a member of the House of Representatives," Alex hissed, not wanting to bring any more attention to their table.

Kita shrugged. "She's a bitch, Alex."

She was. But that was irrelevant. "Dammit, you may not care about your reputation but I have superiors to report to."

Kita shoved out of the booth. Alex tossed a twenty on the table and stomped after her.

She slammed out of the diner, ignoring him. He'd bet his next paycheck she was rolling her eyes at him, but she didn't say a word.

"You can't just go around slinging accusations at elected officials."

She whipped around, fists clenched, eyes blazing. "Something is off with her." She was breathing heavily.

Alex started to argue but he realized she was right. Darla Nichols had deliberately baited Kita. "What's your analysis?"

"I don't know." Her shoulders dropped and she tilted her head back to stare at the crisp fall sky. "She was off though. The other night at the fundraiser she acted a little weird too."

"Weird how?"

"She subtly insisted that the judge stay and she would take him home. She seemed pretty annoyed when Shep insisted that we both leave."

Alex stared down the street at the elegant façade of the Sofitel. His gut churned. "You think a sitting congresswoman has something to do with the threats to the judge."

"I don't know."

"We can't just accuse her." Alex could see his career

circling down the toilet. And yet he knew what she meant. There was something off about the congresswoman.

"I know that." Kita said, "I may be a bit of a rebel but despite my actions in the last ten minutes, I'm not stupid. However, I can follow an evidence trail like a boss. I need to get back to my computer."

"How can someone like Darla Nichols piss you off after you survived your mother?" he blurted out.

Her husky laugh surprised him.

"I was terrified of my mother," Kita said wryly. "Darla Nichols doesn't scare me. She's a pussycat compared to Mommy."

Chapter 17

They'd been studying the case files for the past three hours.

Dwayne, Shep, and the judge were asleep in the three bedrooms, with the judge sandwiched in the middle room. The alarm system was set. Dwayne and Shep were scheduled to take over at midnight and spell Alex and Kita for a six-hour shift. A single bulb lamp in the sparse corner lit the table with intimate shadows.

Kita perched on a folding chair in the dining room, the chair tilted on the back two legs, the front two in the air.

"You're going to fall back and break your neck." The little smirk on his face let her know Alex was teasing. He leaned back and rubbed his neck. "Want to take a break?"

"In a second, let me set up this trace." Kita gripped a pen between her lips, her frown concentrated. There was something there. She just had to find it.

"What are you tracing?"

"Immigration status of Darla Nichol's extended family."

"What?" His voice rose.

"Shh." Kita held up one finger, telling him to wait.

But in her peripheral vision, his face flushed, his hands clenched, and his eyes sparked with temper. His body language distracted her. She could practically see his blood pressure rising. But a little guilt wasn't enough to get her to back off. Something was wonky with Darla Nichols.

"Jesus, Kita."

She tried to distract him. "Don't worry about it. No one will know I was in the system."

"No one will know?!" Alex shout-whispered. "I'll know. Besides which, how can you be sure?"

She had to say it even though she was pretty sure she knew what his response was going to be. "I just am. I think we should go after her."

"We can't just accuse a sitting congresswoman of stalking."

Sadly, he was right.

"What if this is someone who's trying to implicate her, hoping to derail her campaign? If the press got a whiff of our investigation, it would be political death." His face was white.

Also true.

"I still think something is off with her."

"Maybe so, but until we have proof we can't say anything to anyone."

Yeah. But he seemed averse to pursuing the truth. Even quietly. "Relax, Alex." Kita said, "I would never put your career in jeopardy. Why are you so worried about this anyway?"

Alex's jaw flexed. She was pretty sure he was gritting his teeth. "The reason I was moved to the judiciary protection arena was because I'd voiced concern about a witness. He was an informant. He ratted on the mob after his wife was killed."

"You didn't approve of the witness."

"No. I mean, of course I'm not thrilled he was a mob guy. But that wasn't why I didn't approve. It's not my job to agree or disagree about the morality of our witnesses. And I would never let that affect my ability to do my job."

"So what happened?"

"Yeah, I told anyone who would listen that the guy was not a good candidate for the program."

Kita waited patiently.

"I didn't back down but no one agreed with my assessment."

"And?"

"My gut was right. He was killed within two weeks of being relocated." Alex blew out a frustrated breath. "I knew there was no way he was going to cut all contact with his mother."

"So what does that have to do with you blowing a gasket every time I do anything that doesn't appear to follow your rules?"

"I'm on probation right now. I can't afford to have any missteps on this case."

Kita's guilt mushroomed. So much was wrong about the pairing of the two of them. "I'm sorry," she said softly. She put her hand on his forearm.

Attraction zinged up her arm, sizzling through her.

"It's hardly your fault." Alex countered, his muscles flexing beneath her palm, as if he were restraining himself from touching her.

If he knew what ALIAS did, how they tended to skirt laws and hide people, he'd be completely freaking out.

"What?" he asked.

Kita jerked back from him. "Nothing."

"You had a funny look on your face."

"Must have been that cheese I ate for dinner."

He narrowed his gaze and she forced a smile.

"I've been meaning to ask you." Alex redirected back to the conversation. Unfortunately she figured she wouldn't be able to answer truthfully. "What did Marsh's mother mean when she said 'you and your secret projects'?"

Kita blinked.

It was like he'd heard her thoughts.

"No idea." She could feel the flush creeping up her face.

Fortunately, they were interrupted by Dwayne. Saved by the Samoan. Kita wanted to laugh. She'd have to be sure to thank him later.

Dwayne rubbed his face. His huge yawn cracked his jaw as he shuffled toward the never-empty coffeepot. He wore gym shorts, a T-shirt, and a shoulder holster. "Hey." He poured the coffee, which had to be sludge now, into one of the Styrofoam cups. "Shep up yet?"

"Not yet."

"Cool."

Alex went into the kitchen to throw away the garbage from their research session.

While he was in the other room, Dwayne leaned in close to Kita and whispered in her ear. "If you're gonna use any more of those prophylactics, the best bedroom for proper security coverage is the rear one."

Kita whispered back. "What are you talking about?"

"Next time, empty the garbage can."

Oh my God. Serious rookie move.

"Fine," she said grumpily. "But that's not going to be a problem."

Dwayne grinned, his straight white teeth framed by those slightly crooked lips. "Makes no difference to me."

Alex had come back into the dining room and was staring at them distrustfully.

As soon as Shep wandered into the main living area, Kita beat a hasty retreat. "See you in six."

Unfortunately, Alex was right behind her. "What was that about?" He spoke quietly but forcefully.

"Nothing." But she kept her gaze averted. The full body flush started at her toes and bled toward her hairline in a blast of embarrassment.

Alex grabbed her arm as she went through the last bedroom door. She didn't have any desire to sleep in the room they'd used last night.

"It wasn't nothing."

"Fine. You want to know?" Kita rounded on him. "Dwayne reminded me that if we're going to fuck each other we should use this bedroom, so we're still utilizing maximum cover protection for the judge."

Alex reared back, then he tugged her away from the doorway. Quietly, deliberately he closed the door, entombing them in the silent midnight air. Somehow she didn't think it was for sexy times.

Which pissed her off.

Rage pulsed off him in waves.

"What is your problem?" Was he somehow trying to blame her for last night? Kita bunched her fists, shoved up her chin and her shoulders back, bracing for the rejection practically blasting at her.

"You told him?" Alex's gaze burned as he pushed into her personal space, but what left her speechless was the hurt on his face. Kita hesitated, on unsure ground. Yeah, it was slightly embarrassing but she didn't worry about the opinions of others. Except, she cared what he thought about her. Against all reason. She cared. Apparently he did too.

"He saw the condom wrapper," she said quietly.

"Oh." He had the grace to appear embarrassed. "Sorry."

"Is sleeping with me so repulsive then?"

"No. Sorry. I don't know."

No and *sorry* worked. *I don't know*, not so much.

Alex thunked his head softly against the door. "I don't usually have any trouble with following my own rules."

Was he…?

"But with you…" His brilliant eyes pierced her with an intense stare. "I'm having a hard time remembering why this is a bad idea."

It was a bad idea. It was a bad idea the first time they did it. And the more she got to know him, the worse idea it turned into. They were complete opposites. And yet, Kita was equally drawn to him. "I don't typically have a hard time resisting either," she confessed.

Kita glanced away from his penetrating gaze. Unsure, and even unsettled, because it was true. She had never been overcome with lust. As a matter of fact, she'd always thought her friends were just justifying their own weak behavior when they said they couldn't help themselves.

The air in the dark silent bedroom heated, and desire swirled through her like a compulsive craving she couldn't deny. Silence. Awkwardness.

Alex didn't move.

Kita closed her eyes, shutting out her embarrassment. Guess that was what happened when you put yourself out there. "Well, I'll just…go." She pasted a determined smile on her face and stared into his eyes. "See you in the morning."

Before she could move, he seized her shoulders. His

palms heated even through the fabric of her top as he tugged her against his body.

"Tell me this is a bad idea," he whispered against her mouth. Coffee, cream, and that fresh pine scent overwhelmed her.

Her heart thudded in overtime, her lips tingled, and all she wanted was to fall into this kiss. But he followed the rules, and she was not about to lead him into a situation he would regret later. "You know it is."

"It doesn't feel bad," Alex argued. They were so close she could see his ice blue iris circled with a ring of navy. A color that should be cold but instead burned.

Kita routinely circumvented the rules in order to get what she wanted and do her job. She wanted him but not at the expense of his principles.

"Are you trying to convince me or yourself?" she pressed. "Because you know I don't think there's anything wrong with us and sex." She wanted to be blunt.

He skimmed his nose along her neck, the sensual move sending a shiver down her spine. "It feels right."

God, she didn't want to pressure him but each move ramped her arousal higher, and if he wasn't going to come through, she needed to know.

And damn did she want him to come through. "Go with your gut," she groaned.

And he did.

WHAT WAS it about Kita Kim that caused him to lose his damn mind? He knew she wasn't being completely honest with him. Yet every time they got within close proximity, his common sense and every fucking rule he'd ever followed disappeared in a puff of lust.

His gut was telling him to take her while he had the chance. He pressed her up against the wall, his thigh between her legs. Kita practically climbed up his body, rocking her hot sex against the hard muscles of his leg.

The grunts and groans as she moaned into his mouth caused him to grow even harder. Her furtive caresses as she popped the button on his khakis and hurriedly unzipped his pants ramped up his desire. Her fingers wrapped around his cock. His body went from zero to warp speed in a matter of seconds when they came within a foot of each other. She pushed him back so she had room to pump his cock with a sure, determined fist.

Alex nipped at her bottom lip, demanding she open for him. They bumped against the wall as they rocked together.

And fuck, but they needed to be quiet.

Dwayne and Shep were down the hall. The judge was next door. And Alex didn't care. All he could focus on was getting inside her. Faster, Harder. Now.

He lifted her up, away from the wall and carried her to the bed.

Alex ripped her shirt over her head while she shoved his pants and briefs to his ankles. Then they switched, Kita shedding her own pants while Alex flung his shirt over her shoulder. She pushed him to the bed, the springs squeaking as they bounced.

Kita crawled on top of him. "Not this time," he murmured against her mouth.

He rolled, taking her with him until her lithe, supple body lay beneath his hard, aching one.

Someone had left the bag from the hospital with that

condom on the bedside table. He should be conflicted, or at the very least annoyed. "Thank Christ," he whispered.

Alex ripped the packet open while Kita shook against him desperately. Her hair tumbled around her face in a multi-hued cloud. Her lips were puffy and deeply colored from the force of their kisses.

"You're so fucking beautiful."

Alex didn't miss the flash of surprise on her face, but he'd have to address that insecurity later. Because now he needed to be inside her. As if he would die if she didn't suck him in and surround him with her heat and her sexy wantonness.

"Hurry," she begged.

Within economy of movement, he rolled the condom on his throbbing flesh and in one smooth motion he thrust inside her.

Kita gasped. Arched up into his embrace, her nipples stabbing his pecs, and her hips banging into his.

She tucked her head into his neck and bit his shoulder.

Alex tunneled his palms beneath her superior ass and lifted her into his thrusts. With every crash together she tightened around his cock. The sensations were amazing, mind-bending, mind-blowing.

Kita curled her legs around his thighs, her heels digging into his ass. "Harder."

They banged into each other. The force of their coming together moved them across the mattress. Every thrust, their pubic bones smashed together, and his cock massaged that swollen nub inside her. Her channel tightened, and tightened, as he grew bigger and bigger.

Goddammit he was going to blow.

Kita bowed back, her mouth open in a rictus of

pleasure, as her orgasm crashed through her and milked his cock with long hard draws.

The top of Alex's head nearly blew off as exploded in a cascade of pleasure so intense he wasn't sure he'd ever recover.

"Holy shit." He buried his face in her neck, his body so replete he could barely move.

"You've got good instincts," she said breathily.

Chapter 18

The blaring of a cell phone woke him up. Again.

Alex grabbed the phone and pressed the answer button without looking at the screen. "'Lo?"

"Kita! Ms. Kim?"

Alex shook the sleep from his head. The woman was panicked. "Hold on." He nudged Kita's bare shoulder. "Phone."

She shot up in bed. The sheets dropped to her waist, baring her pert breasts. She snatched the phone from his outstretched hand. "Kim."

Kita propped her elbows on her bent knees and ducked her head while she talked. The fall of her hair hid her face, but the tightness in her voice gave away her distress. "Where are you right now?"

Alex listened with increasing worry as she gave the caller directions and set up a meeting near the Amtrak station. Kita wanted the woman to park and wait for her.

Kita hung up and tilted her head back. Her sigh was long, hard, heartfelt.

"What's wrong?"

She jerked as if she'd been shot. "Uh, just a…friend who's got a problem."

Alex wasn't completely naïve. He'd heard enough from the woman's raised voice to know she was in trouble and in danger. Kita didn't want to share, but it sounded like she could use a partner. "Can I help?"

Kita avoided his attention, her focus on their clothes scattered across the scratched hardwood floor. "No, thanks." She shifted and met his gaze head-on. "I've got this."

Something, some gut instinct put him on high alert. "Your friend is in danger."

"Trust me, Alex." Kita began pulling on her yoga pants. "You do not want to get involved."

But Alex didn't like the way she avoided making eye contact. He watched silently from the rumpled bed.

"I've got to go out," Kita said determinedly. "I'll be back before our shift. I promise." She wiggled her fingers, then with a sharp smile she was gone.

It took him less than five minutes to decide to follow her. Shep and Dwayne had the judge situation under control. As long as he and Kita were back by six in the morning they weren't breaking any major rules.

But he did need to let the other two men know where he was going.

"I'm going out." Alex dropped into the folding chair and tugged on his tennis shoes.

Dwayne was watching him, but it was Shep who spoke. "Now you?"

"I'm going to give Kita some backup." If Alex hadn't been staring at Dwayne he might have missed the wince.

"Not a good idea, my man." Dwayne shook his head.

"Why not?"

"Kita can handle herself."

"Maybe so." Alex wasn't going to be deterred. For several reasons. Something else was going on here. It had taken him longer than it should have to figure out that Adams-Larsen was more than just a PR agency. "But I'm going anyway."

His gut was telling him that she might need his help. It was also telling him he might not like what he found.

"I'll be back."

Dwayne just shook his head.

Alex arrived at Union Station. She'd told whoever was on the other end of the phone to meet her in the parking lot near the steps.

He waited in his car impatiently, searching for Dwayne's little Honda Fit. Finally, he saw the smaller car, wondering for a second why a guy that big would have such a small car. But when he found it, the vehicle was empty.

Alex drove around the parking lot until he could find a good vantage point to watch the exit. About five minutes later, Kita strode through the doors and headed toward the parking lot. She held a paper cup with steaming liquid in her hand, which she tossed into a garbage can by the exit without even looking.

Behind her trailed a woman and three young kids.

Alex's jaw dropped. Kids?

Kita hustled the woman and kids into Dwayne's car, jamming all five into the sub compact.

Alex followed behind Kita, using protocol to tail her vehicle.

She began to take evasive maneuvers, doing a standard surveillance detection route, to make sure no one was following her. Except Alex knew what she was doing. But then he started wondering…how did she know what to do? And why did she think evasive action was necessary?

This was ridiculous. He was on her six. Just him. It was three o'clock in the morning. Barely anyone was out this time of night. Even in DC.

Alex punched in her cell number. She picked up on the first ring. "Kim."

"It's me."

"I know who you are." Sarcasm dripped from her voice.

"I meant, I'm in the car behind you."

She drew a sharp breath. "Of course you are. Go home." Which sounded a lot like *Go to hell*.

"Just let me help you." Alex said, "Besides, I have some questions."

"I'm sure you do." Kita sighed.

At that moment, one of the kids let out a mournful wail. The frantic shushing from an adult voice came through loud and clear.

Alex waited, knowing not to push.

"Fine." Kita acquiesced. "Follow me."

She headed toward Alexandria, driving efficiently and at the edge of the speed limit but never going over.

She turned into the parking lot of an eight story apartment building. Once they were both parked, Alex strode over to her car.

Kita jerked out of the car, her face a thundercloud. But when she turned to the woman, who clutched a little girl of maybe two or three to her chest, she spoke gently. "Hannah. No need to be afraid. This is my friend, Alex."

Hannah nodded and ducked her face down, but not before Alex saw the damage. One eye was completely swollen shut. The other was red-rimmed and bloodshot. The arm that wasn't holding the child was tucked tight against her ribcage. She was herding the other kids out of the car but moving extra slowly as if every physical action hurt.

Shit.

The woman's body shook with shivers. She wasn't wearing a coat, even though all three kids had their coats on.

"How can I help?" Alex made his body language nonthreatening.

"If you would bring the bag from the trunk, that would be great." Kita had also lowered her voice. She held the eldest girl's hand and hoisted the other up on to her hip. "Cover us to the entrance?"

Alex pressed his mouth into a tight line to stop the cursing that wanted to burst from his lips. Dammit. *Dammit.*

Cover them. What the hell?

"Sure." He slung a single duffel bag over his shoulder and left his gun hand free. He visually swept the parking lot for any attackers but besides the intermittent swish of traffic from the main street a block over, the area was quiet.

"Looks good." Alex gave Kita the go-ahead.

She nodded. "C'mon girls. Let's have a sleepover."

He'd never heard her voice so perky. Alex followed the women and kids into the building. Kita needed a key for entry into the lobby. Then a key again to get the elevator to rise. Within a few minutes, she opened the door to an apartment.

Kita urged everyone to take their shoes off and leave them on the mat by the front door. Alex left his on.

He closed the drapes while Kita got the woman and kids settled into the single bedroom. In the full light of the apartment's living room, the damage to the woman's face was even more severe.

The kids were subdued, even a little fearful of Alex,

which pretty much confirmed his suspicion that Hannah was a victim of domestic violence. The kids appeared to be unharmed physically. Of course, who knew what their mental state was.

Alex had the nagging sense that the woman looked familiar. Her body movements tugged at his subconscious. Of course, he'd seen abused women before in his line of work but it was more than that.

He let his mind work at the puzzle of Hannah and her kids while he prowled around what he quickly realized was Kita's apartment. Inside the entryway was a fancy mountain bike, several pairs of athletic shoes, and a basket full of sports equipment. A sliding glass door led to a small balcony. A mix of different size pots clustered in each corner. Little rectangular boxes hung from the railing and held a mix of some big pom-pom-type flowers like the girls used to get for homecoming, surrounded by spiky plants and trailing leaves with purple flowers.

He paced the living room, peripherally noting the aesthetic mix of Asian and Western design. A clearly ancient tea service perched next to a small wood box that held the remote control. A squat little Buddha statue smiled happily on the coffee table. In the kitchen, a planter box full of herbs sat on the windowsill. He took note of the little facets of her personality revealed by her furnishings. The small apartment filled with a sense of serenity.

A little while later, Kita came out of the bedroom, her gaze blank. She gave a little sigh, then jerked when she noticed him standing there.

"Oh, uh, hey." Then she ignored him. She sat at the desktop on the elegantly carved antique desk and flipped on the computer.

"That's it?" Alex's temper began to boil. "Hey?"

She didn't even look at him. "You're welcome to have a seat." She gestured at the sofa.

Once the computer booted up, she began clacking away on the keys. She was on the Amtrak website. She bought a one-way ticket for Hannah Smith from DC to Denver, leaving in twenty minutes.

Hannah Smith. Fuck. Now he knew why she looked familiar.

Hannah Smith had been all over the news a few months ago, while they'd been investigating her brother-in-law. Her sister had disappeared and no one had ever found her. Hannah had been very vocal about saying her sister would never leave her children.

"There's no way she can make that train." Alex thought he'd point out the obvious and observe Kita's response.

Kita leaned back in the chair and let out a tense breath. "That would be the point."

And that was when he remembered where else he'd seen Hannah Smith before. "She was the woman you were sparring with the day we met."

Kita nodded sharply.

His brain was swirling. What the hell was going on here? "Those aren't her kids."

"Nope."

Other details clicked into place. "Her coat?"

"Left at the station."

The picture was becoming clearer. "With a receipt for a cup of coffee time-stamped in the pocket?" Pocket litter. Tradecraft 101.

Kita rubbed her face, her weariness apparent.

When she didn't answer, he speculated, "Near the track for the train she isn't going to board."

"That would be the plan."

It was at this moment that Alex realized some key information had been left out of the background he had on Kita, which now that he thought about it was slim. These were not the actions of a damned social media seeder. "Where did you work before Adams-Larsen?"

"I'm not at liberty—"

"Cut the bullshit."

"Fine. I worked for the CIA," Kita said. "But that's all I can tell you."

The CIA. The Central Intelligence Agency. Other little nuggets poked at his brain. The training. The hacking. The reason the judge wanted Adams-Larsen involved in the first place. "What does Adams-Larsen really do?"

"We're a full service image consulting agency."

"I know what your website says," he ground out. "I'm asking *you*."

"I'm sorry." Kita didn't say another word.

But as details clicked in his brain, he was compelled to keep pushing. "The shooting at your offices last month."

"I didn't have anything to do with that."

"But the FBI did." Russians. Top secret. Supposedly the CIA had also been involved. Although that was just rumor in the intelligence community. "Rumor has it that the CIA was there too."

She winced. "I don't know."

"Sergei Polzin was a Russian on the no-fly list who mysteriously got into the US and was somehow shot and killed on Adams-Larsen premises."

"So I've heard."

"Okay, fine. You don't want to talk about that?" Alex began to pace. "Let's talk about why Hannah Smith is in your bedroom."

"It would be best if you forgot you saw her."

Like that was going to happen.

"I'm not leaving until we discuss a few things."

"Well then you're going to be here a long time." Kita crossed her arms and lifted her chin in a big "fuck you." A sharp vulnerability darkened her eyes, and guilt assailed him. He didn't want to hurt her but she was in the wrong here. Not him. But it still made him feel like shit. A grinding nausea churned in the pit of his stomach, but he couldn't let it go.

The woman in the other room. The children. "This is kidnapping."

She just sat there.

Finally, she said, "It's just a matter of time before he starts hitting those kids. Even you, Mr. Rule Follower, can see that Hannah and the children are in danger."

"There are proper channels—" He stopped. Because this wasn't just about principles, although he didn't want anything to happen to the kids, and yes, the wife's disappearance was suspect, but, he couldn't help reiterating, "She doesn't have custody."

"You don't want to continue." Kita pressed her palms together in a gesture of begging. "He killed his wife."

"They couldn't find the proof," Alex shot back. Except these kids were vulnerable.

"There is no way the wife left his kids with him," Kita argued. "He's an abuser and a killer."

"It's still not in your jurisdiction to hide those kids from their father." There were proper channels to protect the kids. "That's why we have laws."

LAWS. Rules. Alex Saunders would never see the exceptions.

But it was what Adams-Larsen did. Except for the fact that Hannah Smith was the girls' aunt and not their mother, she fit the standard profile for the type of clients they helped. But By-The-Book Saunders would not understand that.

This conversation underscored their differences. All the reasons they were a bad idea. The hope she'd secretly let grow and blossom withered.

"You need to go." Kita thought about their connection, the heated touches and whispered words, the feeling that finally she was beginning to relate to a man on another level. One that until recently she didn't even believe was possible.

But Alex Saunders would never approve of her or her methods. That truth festered like a cut flower in decaying water.

And right now, saving Hannah Smith was her top priority.

"Make me understand." He was practically begging her as if he too was mourning the loss of what had grown between them.

But Kita closed off her heart, shut down her feelings. She couldn't afford for him to get in her way. "I'll meet you back at the safe house."

"That's it?" His gaze went flat. "We're not even going to discuss—"

"There's nothing to discuss." She turned her back on him, unable to take the disappointment in his eyes. Because she knew if she explained her real calling, what she did to protect the innocent, the disappointment would only get worse. She'd been judged and found lacking often enough her life. She should have never given him the power to hurt her.

"You're right." Alex opened the door to the apartment hallway. He looked back, his mouth an unsmiling line, disappointment in the sharp lines of his face. "I guess I was wrong and we have nothing."

He closed the door quietly, the click of the lock abnormally loud in her silent apartment.

Kita stood there, in the middle of her living room, and mourned for the loss. She hadn't even realized how much she wanted him to stick around. To say "To hell with the rules and let's do what's right." To believe in her and what she did. To accept her for who she was. All that regret balled in her chest and rose in her throat as she breathed heavily through her pain. She swallowed the urge to weep. Her eyes smarted, and her throat constricted.

But Kita didn't have time.

She'd set up the false trail for Frank Donner and the police, assuming he got them involved. Kita needed to take pictures of Hannah but she'd wait until morning. The woman needed sleep.

Now she needed to make a phone call she was dreading.

She pulled out her cell and dialed Jill.

"Larsen," Jillian answered crisply. But Kita knew she'd woken her up.

"Hey."

It was almost comical how Jill anticipated things. "What did you do?"

"He beat her up. Bad."

"Kita?"

She sighed. "She's in my apartment."

Silence. "Okay. Give me an hour. I'd already started putting a plan in place."

Relief and gratitude nearly overwhelmed her. There was a knock at Kita's front door and she used the interruption to swallow her feelings. "Hold on. Someone is at my door."

"You can't answer it," Jill said.

"Relax. It's probably Alex."

"Do I want to know why you think Alex Saunders is at your door at 4 a.m.?"

"I'd guess not." Kita put the phone down by her side so she couldn't hear Jill yell at her. Even so she was distracted as she yanked open the door.

Shit. It wasn't Alex. She stared at the barrel of the very lethal gun pointed at her, and took a step back.

"Hello, Ms. Kim."

Shit.

Darla Nichols held the handgun very competently.

Kita could hear Jill in the background. Her first thought as she stared at that gun? She couldn't afford to resist. The girls shouldn't have to handle any more violence. She wasn't sure Hannah had much left to give either. The best thing she could do was go with Darla Nichols and disarm her once they were away from the apartment.

"It's a little early for a social call, Congresswoman Nichols." She had to speak loud enough for Jill to hear her but not too loud. The last thing she needed was for Hannah to come out of her bedroom.

Kita had to give the congresswoman props. Kita's location wasn't that easy to find.

"Let's go." Darla Nichols gestured with the gun.

Kita's second thought was that she'd never admitted to Alex how much he'd changed her view of relationships. And how much she appreciated him. Not to be morbid and, jeez, she should be able to fight Darla Nichols. But she knew that her survival was not guaranteed.

Darla Nichols didn't know that she worked for ALIAS. That was a plus. She thought she was the judge's aide so she wouldn't be expecting Kita to fight back.

She also hadn't seen Kita's phone in her hand. Kita hoped that Jill caught some of this conversation.

"Is the gun really necessary?"

"Don't make me shoot you."

Kita shut her mouth.

She tucked the phone between her waistband and the small of her back. The worst fucking place for it but hopefully Darla wouldn't pat her down.

Just in time too.

Darla tossed her a zip tie. "Bind your wrists."

Well, that put a damper on her escape plans. Kita kept quiet, praying that Hannah and the kids were sound asleep and wouldn't come to investigate. Getting the PlasticCuff on was awkward, and she attempted to keep the plastic relatively loose.

"Tighten it with your teeth."

Foiled again.

Chapter 19

Alex had just walked in the door of the safe house when his phone rang. He glanced at the display. Jillian Larsen. He was tempted to ignore the call. With a sigh, he pressed the answer button. "Saunders."

"How close are you to Kita's apartment?" Jillian Larsen bulleted out.

Why would Kita tell Jillian he'd been at her apartment? "I fail to see how—"

"Congresswoman Nichols just abducted Kita at gunpoint."

Alex's heart stopped. A frigid cold swirled around him. "She could kick her ass. Why would she just go with her?"

"I'm assuming it has to do with the additional cargo in her bedroom."

Shit. She'd done it to protect Hannah Smith… "Or did she do it to protect Adams-Larsen?" Alex asked cynically.

"Saunders. We hired Kita because, despite her aversion to rules, she has a giant heart."

Shit. He knew that. Shame funneled through him. "What do you need me to do?"

"I'm on my way to Kita's apartment." Alex could hear the screech of her tires through the line. "Where are you?"

Suddenly all the other stuff fell away. They could argue the merits of right versus wrong or gray versus gray all day, but at the end of it, he wanted to snuggle up to Kita in bed and savor her.

He wanted Kita, all of her. Even the obstinate pieces he didn't necessarily agree with. Which meant he needed to find her. Save her.

Okay. She could save herself, but he could at the very least help. "We need to figure out where Darla Nichols would take her. And why. Is this about the judge?"

"We need to see if the GPS tracker on her phone is transmitting. Maybe then we can figure out where they are going."

"Give me the info," Alex said.

Jillian hesitated. "Can I trust you—"

"Jillian. I will do anything for her," Alex vowed.

"Fair enough. I'll be at her apartment taking care of our other issue."

Crazy thoughts careened through his mind, battering at him. He couldn't lose her. He couldn't.

Why would Darla take Kita?

Shit. He should have never ignored his gut.

He'd actually agreed with Kita that the congresswoman had seemed to be hiding something. But he hadn't wanted to pursue her aggressively because of the high-profile stink it would have caused. And because seriously, what were the odds that an elected public official would actually be stalking a federal judge? And he still had no idea why.

Now the crazy bitch had Kita.

Alex's stomach cramped.

What was Darla's motivation? Did she think Kita was

somehow obstructing her chances with the judge? Except the congresswoman had been clear during their interview that she was merely looking to the judge for help in her career. Of course, she could have been lying.

She was fucking Judge Adams for recommendations on the subcommittee on foreign affairs. It wasn't clear whether the judge truly intended to back her. The other pertinent question went back to the beginning of the investigation. Why had the judge insisted on bringing in ALIAS?

Alex strode into the living room. Shep and Dwayne looked up. "We need to wake up the judge. I need to talk to him."

"What?"

"Congresswoman Nichols just abducted Kita at gunpoint. I want to know everything he knows about the congresswoman and I need to know yesterday."

"Jesus. Okay." Shep said, "Talk to Dwayne while I wake him up."

"Listen, don't worry. Kita can hold her own. She kicks ass." Dwayne's deep rumble irritated him. But when Alex looked at the large man, worry made his continually smiling face somber.

"But in a fight, if the opponent brings a gun, her odds are significantly reduced."

Dwayne's face blanched. "She is a badass." But he spoke as if he were trying to reassure himself, not just Alex. "We need to come up with a plan to get her back."

No hesitation. Warmth filled Alex. The immediate response from ALIAS was to rescue their coworker. After his mess with the last witness, some of his colleagues had distanced themselves from him, as if worried that his disciplinary sanctions might rub off on them. But the Adams-Larsen team pulled together without hesitation.

Should he call his boss?

He thought for a moment, then rejected the idea. She wouldn't want to save Kita. That would go against protocol. Technically Alex's responsibility was the judge, not his partner.

And that made Alex want to lose his mind.

Finally, the judge shuffled out to the living room. In old-fashioned pajamas with bedhead, the judge was just an old man.

"Why would Congresswoman Nichols kidnap Kita?"

"What?"

"Don't play dumb, old man." Alex had had enough.

The judge sputtered. "I can't believe Darla—"

Alex grabbed the judge by the lapels of his stuffy pajamas and half lifted him onto his toes. "I need answers." He shook the judge, spittle from his mouth landing on the older man's cheek.

In the back of his mind he knew he was out of control, but all he could focus on was the fact that Kita was in harm's way. Nothing else mattered.

Shep peeled his fingers off the judge. "Why don't we all just take a moment to calm down?"

"I don't want to calm the fuck down. I want Kita safe."

Alex's heart thundered in his chest, the beat like a death knell. What if they couldn't find her in time?

Something Darla had said resonated in his mind. "Is she connected to your son in some way?"

"Marsh?" Bobby Adams had backed up and dropped onto the folding chair next to Dwayne. He smoothed down his rumpled hair. "As far as I know they've never met."

"I can look and see if they met in an official capacity." Dwayne flipped open the laptop in front of him.

"Do it."

"Why did you want Adams-Larsen on this operation?" If the judge hadn't insisted, Kita wouldn't be in danger right now.

The judge flushed. "I wanted to see my son. He…avoids me."

Alex shook off the urge to punch the judge. His family problems were not the issue. "What about how you hooked up with Nichols? How did that happen? She's older than most of your regular woman." Except for Joyce Nguyen and Colleen Adams. Okay, shit, maybe that was a dead end too.

The judge blinked as if consulting some document only he could see. "She approached me."

"And you didn't find that suspicious? You strike me as the kind of guy who makes his own conquests." Without waiting for an answer, Alex changed his line of questioning. "Why do you think Darla targeted you?"

"I have the connections to get the appointments she wants."

"So you slept with her?"

"Let's not get judgmental. It's a game," Judge Adams said. "That's politics. You play the game or you lose. Those are the rules."

Fuck their rules. Alex wanted to show the judge his right hook.

Shep wrapped his hand around Alex's biceps. "Ah, Alex. You may want to tone it down a bit." He tried to pull Alex back a step.

"Yeah. No. I don't. What I want is to figure out why a sitting congresswoman just kidnapped a woman who has ties to the judge and to his son. Darla doesn't know that Kita isn't your aide. She still thinks she's working for you but her interest took an unhealthier turn when she learned that Kita knew Marsh."

"Well, that's bizarre." The judge finally said, "Why would she care about Marsh?"

"Exactly," Alex said through a jaw so tight his teeth might crack.

"Darla Nichols took over her husband's house seat when he died a month into his second term."

"And none of this history lesson is helping us figure out where she took Kita." Alex had to wonder if there was some sort of connection. "How did he die?"

"Heart attack," Dwayne interjected.

"Hardly grounds for revenge." So as far as Alex could see there wasn't a correlation.

"Jesus, we've been working under the radar for five years and all of a sudden within a month we've got two high-profile problems." Dwayne rubbed his chin.

Finally, Alex had another line to pursue. "What does Adams-Larsen really do?"

Dwayne sat hyper still. "What are you talking about?"

"Kita is former CIA. Jillian and Marsh are former marshals. I'm betting you used to work for another agency. None of those agencies are particularly known for their public relations skills." Alex couldn't keep the rage out of his voice. "My guess, whatever her grudge is with Marsh has to do with your real business."

Dwayne looked away. "Our image consulting business doesn't have anything to do with why Kita was abducted."

"You'd better hope that whatever you're withholding doesn't have the power to save her." Alex wanted to punch something. Dwayne was handy. Except they'd need everyone to rescue Kita.

"I would never do anything to put a woman, especially Kita, in jeopardy." Dwayne spoke with a sincerity that couldn't be missed.

He had to think. Alex crouched in the chair, and put his head in hands, going over all the data from the past few days. "She's Russian. The Russian guy was killed in your office. Could she somehow be connected to the guy who was killed at Adams-Larsen?"

"I can't imagine," the judge said.

"I've got her." Dwayne raised his fists in triumph.

"Where is she?" The edge of the keys dug into his palm.

The computer dinged again. Dwayne said, "Wait a minute."

"What's going on?"

Dwayne was silent. "Kita's trace on Darla Nichols's dossier finally came through. There are anomalies in the congresswoman's background."

"Anomalies?" the judge said at the same time as Alex.

"What kind of anomalies?" All this talking wasn't getting them any closer to Kita.

"The setup of her accounts, identity, backstop. Not all of her official details can be verified." Dwayne was peering intently at the screen. "Jesus, it's manufactured."

"Which parts?"

"It will take forever to dig into it." Dwayne continued to scroll through the report on the screen. "Whoever did this is *good*."

Alex didn't give a good goddamn. "What does this mean for Kita?"

The judge perked up. "When did Darla meet her husband?"

"Sophomore year of college." Even Alex knew this. "They met at a political rally. They both volunteered on their local candidate's campaign."

"A few years ago, the FBI arrested a ring of Russian

spies who were to infiltrate society and spy on citizens with ties to certain industries."

Alex nodded. "I remember the case. Operation Ghost Stories."

Dwayne's eyebrows lifted. "There were rumors that not everyone in the ring was caught. That there were actually sleepers who'd been sent much earlier in life and had undergone programming to appear like ordinary US citizens. But that was never proven, and the Russian government denied any additional personnel associated with the ring."

Alex couldn't wrap his mind around what Dwayne was insinuating. "You think Darla Nichols is a Russian spy?"

"Think about the genius of it," Judge Adams said with admiration. "She studies law and marries an up-and-coming politician. Once he hits the House, she kills him, takes over, and then influences American policy."

Alex thought they'd detoured right into cray-cray land. "Are we really going there?"

"Looks like her grandmother raised her." Dwayne read from his screen. "She emigrated from Siberia."

Impatience rose to the surface, bubbling through him with beats of urgency. This felt like a complete waste of time. "Why does that matter?"

"Because the Russian on the no-fly list who was killed at Adams-Larsen last month was from there too," Dwayne said grimly.

"Russia is a huge country. Get to the fucking point." Alex wanted to tear his hair out.

"But this particular section near Lake Baikal is small and very tight knit."

So this was some sort of retaliation for the death of the Russian at Adams-Larsen?

Alex's phone rang. It was Jill. "What?"

"Well, we heard from the congresswoman. She knew Kita still had her phone," Jill said. "We've got a big problem."

"Why?"

"She wants Marsh."

Okay, well he knew that Marsh had been gone for a month. Their original speculation that the person writing the letters wanted Marsh appeared to be dead-on.

Marsh Adams could hopefully make this whole thing go away. With as close as the employees at Adams-Larsen seemed to be, and the fact that he was Kita's childhood friend, his compliance should be a no-brainer. "Well, then. Get. Him."

"We can't." Jillian finished before he could rip her fucking head off. "He's missing."

Chapter 20

K ita had her hands full driving with the plastic zip tie on her wrist. Darla Nichols, AKA crazy bitch, sat in the backseat behind her. "I will shoot you if you slow down." They were on the Beltway heading toward Rock Creek Park. Well, that minimized her options, didn't it? There was no way to roll from the car going this fast.

The good news was, once they stopped and were out of the car, Kita would have the advantage. And at this time of morning, she wouldn't have to worry about collateral damage.

The park should be empty.

"What do you want with Marsh?" Her stomach rocked.

All she needed was a distraction, but so far Darla had been surprisingly tactical. Kita had never gotten close enough to take her down. Which begged the question, was it accidental or was she trained?

"That bastard. I can't wait to make him pay for what he did," Darla muttered.

"What did he do?"

"I want you to die, you know," she said conversationally.

Her lack of emotion made the statement that much more chilling. Darla Nichols wasn't bothered by the thought of murder.

"I still don't understand why."

"Marsh Adams took someone from me. So I want to take someone from him."

Kita was extremely confused. "Who did he take from you?" Maybe that's where Marsh had been? But oh, fuck, if Crazy McCrazyPants was demanding Marsh meet them, Kita was in deep shit. Because according to Jillian, Marsh was MIA.

"Pull into that parking space." They'd arrived at the park. It was o dark thirty and the park was deserted.

Right now, Darla was ignoring Kita. It would be best if she could disarm the woman before someone showed up. Marsh wasn't going to show, obviously. The only other option was to send someone in his place.

She should be upset but right now she was just happy because they couldn't send Alex. Darla had met Alex so he wouldn't be out.

"He killed my lover."

Oookay. Now Kita was really confused. "When did this happen?"

"Last month, you idiot."

The only memorable event last month was the death of Sergei Polzin at ALIAS headquarters. Except he'd been killed by an FBI agent. The press had been given limited information, with the only details being that an unidentified person was in a shootout with Polzin after he took hostages at their office.

"You realize you're burning bridges here. What about your congressional seat?"

"It's over. They're going to find out I poisoned my

husband." Darla laughed bitterly. "My opponent got ahold of a report that was supposed to be destroyed."

"So you're going to prison."

Darla Nichols was silent, clearly thinking.

"Not if I can help it." Darla tapped the headrest.

"Super confused right now, Congresswoman." Kita tried to appeal to her vanity. "Can you explain?"

"Huh. There's an idea."

Kita had no clue what she was talking about but hopefully if she kept the woman distracted she could figure out a way out of this mess.

"Adams-Larsen is going to help me beat this. I'm the innocent victim of a frame job." Darla punched in a number on her cell.

Kita could hear the phone ringing. She wondered who Darla was calling now.

"Good morning, judge," Darla said pleasantly, as if she were making a social call. "I woke up horny," she purred. "Come pay me a visit."

Kita heard the judge blustering in the background. But the tap on his phone meant everyone was listening. She thought about yelling out something to warn him and his security. But the gun pressed up to the back of the seat was a deterrent.

Hopefully Jill had alerted everyone that Darla "Crazy Woman" Nichols had taken her hostage.

"Come on, darling. Have a little adventure."

When the judge agreed, Kita knew that Jill had gotten the information to Alex and Shep. Otherwise there's no way they would have agreed to let him near Darla at this time of night.

She gave him their location. "See you soon, darling."

As soon as she hung up, her voice turned hard. "Let's go."

"It's cold out," Kita whined. She didn't want to make it too easy for the congresswoman. She'd get suspicious otherwise.

"Do it. Or we will have a problem."

Kita reluctantly opened her car door. Darla was standing outside the open door, within kicking distance, and her gun was nowhere to be seen.

Kita kicked out, hitting the woman in the stomach. She grunted but didn't go down. As Kita rolled out of the driver's seat, Darla grabbed her arm. Which would have worked in Kita's favor, except a small pinch on the inside of her arm was the only warning she had.

Immediately her vision began to blur. She opened her mouth and forced out the words, but her tongue had thickened and her eyelids began to droop. "Whaat did youooooo give meeee?"

"Nighty-night."

Fuuuuccccckkk.

ALEX SLAMMED his fist against the scarred tabletop. "We don't have a choice." If it came down to the judge and Kita, he couldn't even go there.

Jillian was on the other end of the line. "Dwayne is too big, and Shep's coloring is all wrong. You're the same general size as Marsh."

"She'll know as soon as she sees me." Alex did not want to put Kita in jeopardy.

But he'd lost the argument. They plotted out a rescue

strategy while Alex was on his way to the park. The judge and Dwayne were right behind him.

He was driving Shep's car. He'd dropped Shep off about a half mile away. He was running to get in place. Fortunately, they still had the tech available from the night of the fundraiser so they could communicate with each other.

Jillian had taken Hannah and the kids to Adams-Larsen and called Maria Torres to keep them company, just in case Frank Donner somehow found out that Kita had been harboring the kids and his sister-in-law. Which, based on the way this evening or morning had turned into a total goatfuck, seemed very likely.

He drove slowly, the headlights cutting through the dark woods. The urge to speed down the road thumped through him like a heavy bass.

He nearly vibrated with the need to get to her. To make sure she was okay. Dwayne and Jill had told him to calm down, that Kita could take care of herself, but until he held her in his arms, he couldn't shake the worry that something was about to go horribly wrong.

He pulled into the parking lot. On the far side, Kita was sitting on a bench with Darla standing behind her. Something was wrong with Kita. He could tell immediately that she was…off.

He pulled the baseball cap low over his brow so that in the still of the night, only his jaw and mouth would be visible.

"In position," Shep said in his ear. "But the way she's standing, if I shoot, there's a possibility the weapon in her hand will go off. At that range, Kita will be dead."

Besides, Darla Nichols was a sitting congresswoman, and

they couldn't just shoot her down in cold blood. As much as Alex wanted to end this and get Kita safe.

"Don't shoot," he murmured. But he couldn't seem to see any way out of this clusterfuck without someone getting shot. "Try to get closer."

"Come on out," Darla called in a singsong-y voice.

Alex exited the car slowly. Put his hands in the air. He was the decoy. "I'm unarmed. Just like you demanded." His voice came out strained. Hopefully Darla had never met Marsh in person. No one seemed certain on that detail, which was a pretty big fucking detail to get wrong.

Darla Nichols held the weapon to Kita's ear. The coffee he'd sucked down sloshed in his stomach, acid churning.

Kita sat docilely, her wrists cuffed in front, her eyes glazed. "What's wrong with her?"

"Benzodiazepine."

Dammit. Alex ran through what he knew about the drug. Sedative, hypnotic, sleep-inducing, anti-anxiety, anticonvulsant, and muscle relaxant properties. Would she be okay? Why hadn't they asked if she was allergic to any other medicines?

"What do you want?"

"I wanted you to pay," she shouted.

He didn't understand. She seemed to have some personal grudge against Marsh Adams. "What for?"

"You killed Sergei!" she screamed.

Who the hell was Sergei?

"This is classified information," Jillian spoke in his ear. "Sergei Polzin was shot in our offices. But Marsh didn't kill him. The bigger question is how she knows about Sergei."

The situation was clearly volatile. "How do you know Sergei?"

"It doesn't matter."

Alex had been hoping to distract her so that Shep could sneak up behind her. But her hand remained steady.

The limousine with the judge and Dwayne drove up. They were out of time.

Alex was this close to giving the order to take her down. The fallout might destroy him but Kita would be safe. Alive.

Chapter 21

K ita's head lolled to the side.

She needed to shake off this sluggishness from whatever drug Darla had given her. Rookie move. A big mistake on her part to underestimate her opponent.

She'd assumed Darla was just a woman who'd taken over her husband's congressional seat, but clearly there was more going on here.

The barrel of Darla's .38 dug into the side of her head. And it *hurt*. She needed to focus, to use that pain to get her head clear. The judge was on his way and she had to protect him.

Their job, Alex's job, was to keep the judge safe.

But Alex was out there, pretending to be Marsh. And when Darla figured out that Alex was the one wearing that Nationals baseball cap, all hell was going to break loose.

Darla was unpredictable, at best.

Unstable, at worst.

Unfortunately, Kita was not processing very quickly. Her body was lethargic. She needed to get the drug through her bloodstream, but when she tried to move her arms nothing happened.

She squeezed her hands into fists, but her motor skills were so compromised that she mostly just curled her fingers in on her palms. Her legs jerked out, kicking a pine cone across the hard-packed ground.

Pine needles scented the air, reminding her of Alex. Alex didn't deserve the fallout from this weird confluence of events. He had done everything by the book. She was the one who went off script and endangered both the judge and her coworkers.

She couldn't let anything happen to Marsh's father.

She had to make this better. She'd made the mess, now it was time for her to clean it up.

But damn she still had very limited range of motion and fine motor capabilities.

She tried to move her legs, and touched another pine cone. Closing her eyes, she focused on lifting her leg just enough to rest her foot on the pine cone.

She pressed down hard, and the sharp edges dug into the soft arch of her bare right foot. Spikes of pain shot up her leg. The pain helped her focus.

Darla was yelling at the judge to get out of his car.

The judge opened his door. In a smart move, he'd positioned his car so that the door protected most of his body. He stood there with only his shins and his neck and his head exposed. Which was still problematic if Darla's shooting ability was as good as her captive-taking skills.

If Kita could just give him some sort of signal so he ducked, the heavy car door would protect him.

Dwayne was the driver of the limousine.

"What is going on here?" The judge's voice trembled. And for the first time since Kita met him, he sounded old.

"Your son is going to pay." Darla threatened. "Initially I wanted to kill someone who mattered."

"You really were going to kill me?" The judge sounded so surprised.

"Yes, legions of women would have wept at your funeral Bobby," she said drily.

He seemed at a total loss for words.

She turned away from the judge and spoke to "Marsh" again. "But I realized that threatening to kill your father or your friend—" she had a hank of Kita's hair in her hand and shook her head like a rag doll, making her scalp sting "—still wouldn't make you pay enough, and I'll still be vulnerable."

"So what are you doing with her like that?" The fake Marsh had barely looked at her. She knew it was Alex and she was terrified that Darla was going to figure it out and shoot him.

She wasn't the most stable person.

"Leverage." Darla said, "If you don't take my threat seriously, you won't do what I want."

Kita guessed the goal was to apprehend Darla alive. But if Darla began to shoot, Kita had to be ready to help.

"So you aren't going to hurt them?" Alex tried to clarify.

"I won't if you agree to help me. If you don't, I have nothing to lose by killing them both."

"What demands?" Alex spoke at the same time the judge said, "I've promised to put in a good word for you, my dear."

"A good word isn't going to cut it." Darla's arm trembled. "Adams-Larsen is going to give me a new identity."

Kita still didn't have enough range of motion. But she

knew she had to move soon. She had to stop this train wreck before the judge got hurt.

"OH HELL." Jill's voice in his ear struck a chord.

"What is she talking about?" Darla Nichols was rambling about starting a new life. The woman had gone completely fucking nuts.

"Who are you running from?" the judge asked. He didn't laugh. He didn't even look confused.

And Jillian's swear word softly echoed in his ear made him realize that he was the only one in this scenario who thought the congresswoman was crazy.

She laughed harshly. "Who isn't after me?"

Alex was trying to catch up, not having a clue what was happening. But suddenly all the little details about Adams-Larsen were clicking into place. The PR firm that didn't seem to have a lot of clients. The ex-CIA and ex-FBI and ex-Marshals. They weren't running a PR firm.

Darla continued, "Marsh took away my ticket out of here."

"You were planning on leaving the country with Sergei Polzin?" The judge tried to keep her attention on him. Probably thinking he was protecting Alex. But Darla was unstable enough that they were all in danger.

"You give people new identities?" Alex asked Jillian. He was trying hard not to move his lips. The last thing they needed was for Darla Nichols to figure out he was wearing a comm device.

"Can we talk about this later?" Jill sounded exasperated.

"I need details if I'm going to negotiate with her."

"Yes. We set up people in the general public who have... problems," Jillian said in his ear.

Betrayal, sharp and intense, burned beneath his breastbone. "This is information I could have used yesterday." But he didn't have time to indulge in anger. At least not right now. Right now he had to save Kita.

Alex bluffed, calling out to Darla Nichols. "We need to know who is after you in order to figure out your logistics."

"Once the news that I killed my husband is made public, the Russians will be after me."

The Russians.

"Explain." Alex barked out.

"I was part of the 'illegals' program as a child. It was started by the SVR, Russian Intelligence."

"Holy shit," whispered Dwayne. "This is what we talked about."

The incident had created a major diplomatic embarrassment between Russia and the US.

"I thought they rounded up all the people in Operation Ghost Stories."

"There are many foreign agents still placed here." Darla laughed. "My grandmother was sent here with the express orders to train her offspring."

"And your mission was to infiltrate the US Government?"

She'd been trying to get on the House Committee on Foreign Relations. So she could influence policy for and against Russian allies and enemies?

"I grew up here, went to college, joined political organizations and began to target individuals with national political aspirations."

The plan was brilliant.

"I married my husband, encouraged him to discuss his positions and his decisions. Once he'd cemented his position in the House of Representatives, I was tasked with eliminating him and taking over his seat." She spoke so dispassionately. Calmly relating that she'd killed her husband of twenty years.

The judge said with wonder, "A sleeper. I wondered about the husband. The timing of his death was definitely suspect."

"Are there more like you?"

"I don't know them. But yes, of course."

Alex dropped his gaze to Kita, checking in with her. She was looking far more alert. But her face still held a groggy cast.

"You're loyal to the Russian government?"

"I may have been born here, but I have served my mother country for many years."

"So that's why you need a new identity?"

"Yes. Once my opponent releases the report that confirms I killed my husband, I will go to prison."

"Why not go to Russia?"

"They are going to be angry with me that I have lost my position in the House." She shook her head. "I cannot go there either."

She pressed the weapon harder to Kita's head.

Kita whimpered.

Alex stared at that weapon, his emotions a churning mass. Protocol insisted they wait for the US Marshals backup. He had called right before they got here. They were coming but he couldn't afford to wait. He stared at Kita, willing her to look at him.

She finally blinked and locked on to his gaze.

Trust me.

But he couldn't say the words out loud. Couldn't afford to let Darla know that he had no intention of honoring her request. That his only motivation was to get Kita to safety.

He didn't even care about the judge anymore.

"I have heard the rumors about Adams-Larsen." Darla Nichols demanded, "You are going to give me a new identity. If you don't, I will kill her."

"Are you the one who threatened me?" The judge's voice shook.

"Yes." Darla sneered. "Agree to help me, Marsh Adams, and your father and friend will live. If not, I will kill them both."

Shep was sneaking up behind Darla. Alex was still concerned that the gun could go off while Shep disabled her. Alex racked his brain for a way to alert Kita that they were about to take her down.

"Why the attacks on the judge? The poisoned drink, the fake anthrax?"

"I was trying to get to you, but you didn't show up. I needed you to show," Darla complained. "But you kept sending your minions." In that moment her concentration wavered.

Three things happened at once.

Shep took a step toward Darla and a branch snapped.

Unable to wait any longer, Alex rushed toward the bench where Kita sat, his weapon in his hand. If he had to shoot the congresswoman, he would. Nothing was more important than Kita's safety.

Darla's attention shifted to Alex. Her eyes widened in shock when she saw his face up close. "You! Where's Marsh?"

Her arm had automatically followed her gaze, and the momentary distraction cost her.

At the same time, Kita wrapped her hands around the congresswoman's wrist, shifted her weight, and threw the woman over her shoulder.

Kita yelled at the judge to duck, and he dove into the interior of the limo.

Darla Nichols landed on the hard ground with a bone-jarring thud.

Kita followed her, wrestling for the gun. The report of the weapon was extremely loud in the early morning mist.

Kita grunted and banged Darla's gun hand repeatedly on the ground, but she was hampered by slow reflexes and her bound wrists.

Shep jumped over the bench and was finally able to wrestle the weapon away from Darla Nichols.

Shep hauled the congresswoman to her feet as she fought valiantly. "Unhand me."

Alex rushed toward the grappling pair, trying to rescue Kita. But she'd already rescued herself.

He bent down and lifted Kita up. Her knees dipped and Alex caught her before she fell, circling his arms around her.

"Are you okay?"

"Still weak. Drugged." Her words slurred as she dropped her forehead against the ball of his shoulder.

"What the hell were you thinking?" He wanted to shake her. He wanted to wrap her in his arms and never let go. He wanted to lock her in a room where she couldn't get into any more trouble.

"Following the rules," she said softly.

"What rules?"

"Protecting the judge," Kita said. "That was our job. *Your* job."

"Not at the expense of your life."

"Couldn't let the judge get hurt," she whispered. "Colleen would be devastated."

Jesus. "Yes. But these were extenuating circumstances."

"All good," she said, "Judge is safe. Your job is safe. We followed the rules."

Fuck the rules.

But before he could tell her so, she dropped into a dead faint.

Chapter 22

The FBI had come and gone.

Darla Nichols was under arrest on multiple counts: kidnapping and drugging Kita, making threats against a federal judge, and the murder of her husband. The FBI would have to verify the truth about her statement that she was a foreign national agent in the Russian government's illegals program.

If that was the case, then Operation Ghost Stories was going to have to be reopened or revisited.

The thought that other Russian sleepers had infiltrated the United States Congress gave everyone the heebie-jeebies.

She had confessed to using AirBNB to rent an apartment in the Watergate on the floor above the judge's co-op. She'd dropped the fake letter on his doormat, knocked on the door, and run up the stairs into the rented apartment.

She'd also been the one to suggest to Vanessa that the US Marshals get involved. She'd basically orchestrated the entire situation for the outcome she'd wanted. And she might have been successful if her opponent hadn't gotten ahold of the autopsy of her husband and exposed her deceptions, prompting her attempts to save herself.

The mystery of the judge's threats was tied up to everyone's satisfaction. Alex's boss wasn't happy that he and Shep had failed to notify the office before they went to rescue Kita. And they might have left out a few pertinent details.

But right now, Alex Saunders had more pressing concerns.

Kita was checked out by Viktor Kuznets, Adams-Larsen's onsite medical guy. Alex was hard-pressed to let go of her. He held her hand while Kuznets did a full exam to make sure she wasn't suffering any more than ill effects from the benzodiazepine.

Alex gave his statement to the FBI. Jillian Larsen smoothed the way and Alex was allowed to stay with Kita as long as he didn't upset her.

He was a little put out by that. Jillian Larsen only said two things to him. "You are under orders not to reveal any of what you learned this morning."

Alex nodded.

Jillian admonished. "All the information is classified."

"Fine."

But that got him to thinking. Because the way her stare bored into him, he had a feeling she wasn't just talking about Darla Nichols being a spy. Jillian indicated that Adams-Larsen was acting with the full consent, or the dubious consent, of some form of the government.

"Anything else?" He wanted to make sure he didn't break any more of her rules.

She smiled but it was lethal. "If you hurt her, I will hunt you down."

And kill you was left unsaid.

"Fair enough."

All the revelations of the morning bombarded him as he sat by Kita's bedside, and she drifted in and out of consciousness. By ten in the morning, the Adams-Larsen office was bustling.

Dwayne checked on Kita repeatedly. Every single time he bussed her forehead and whispered she was a badass. Jillian squeezed her hand every hour she'd checked in. Maria Torres stood in the doorway staring at Kita with regret and a peculiar longing. Some guy named Jake called and talked to Viktor even though he couldn't make it in. Marissa and Bliss from the Adams-Larsen West Coast office —who knew they even had a West Coast office—FaceTimed Kita, talking to her even though she didn't respond. The entire ALIAS family, with the notable exception of Marshall Adams, checked on Kita to make sure she was doing okay.

Alex held her hand the entire time, ignoring the speculative looks from her coworkers and praying for her to wake up.

No one could believe that Kita had stayed conscious long enough to take down the congresswoman. But Kuznets promised she'd wake eventually.

Finally, her eyelids fluttered.

Alex squeezed her fingers gently when she opened her eyes.

For a moment, her gaze was disconcertingly blank. Then awareness returned and a flush spread over her cheeks.

"Hey."

"Hey," she rasped out. "What are you doing here?"

He had no fucking idea. All he knew was that he needed to be here. With her. Making sure she was okay.

"Keeping you in line," he teased. Except he didn't feel like teasing. He'd been worried sick. "What the hell were you thinking?"

She closed her eyes, took a breath. "I was thinking that our job was to protect the judge."

"You could have been killed."

She hesitated. "I didn't want Marsh and Colleen to lose him. He might not be my idea of a good father or a good husband, but they love him."

Anger flashed through him. That was great and all, but, "What about the people who love you?"

KITA WAS FEELING A LOT BETTER. Her strength and sanity returned in a rush when Alex started grilling her.

She could get up. Leave. The conversation was definitely on the uncomfortable side. *What about the people who love you?*

"It's a pretty small list."

Marsh. His mother. That was it. But the sacrifice in that moment had felt like it was worth it to keep them happy.

"Pretty sure it's growing." Alex ducked his head as if he were unsure of her response. The blue-black of his hair dulled in the odd lighting of ALIAS's training room, where they went to get patched up if they had a minor injury.

"I used to believe if I broke the rules, it was all on me." Kita sat up quickly, cupped his face in her palms. "But lately someone made me realize that the rules can have merit."

"But you need to trust your gut too," Alex countered.

She blinked. That was not the response she expected. "I

was afraid that if I put my trust in someone, they could abuse it, and me."

"I would never do that."

She knew they were no longer talking about work. But she still couldn't ask the questions that circled in her mind. Right now she just wanted to get out of the office and take a day or so to recover.

Alex said, "Let's go home."

"Home?"

"I thought we could swing by your place, water your plants." A smile broke out over her face—he got the fact that she wouldn't want her plants to suffer. "Then I could take you to my house. I'll take care of you until you're feeling better."

Her smile widened, her cheeks lifting so hard, it almost hurt. A lightness that had been missing filled her heart with joy. "You want to take me home?"

"I want to take care of you."

She thought about it. They barely knew each other. But she knew the important things. Like he'd be there if she fell and she'd be there if he faltered.

Within a few minutes, he had her bundled up and was ready to carry her to his car. Jillian stopped by to check on her before she left.

"You okay?"

She glanced at Alex. "Better than."

Jill's eyes filled with relief. "I'm glad."

"Uh, yeah. Me too."

Alex said, "I'll bring the car around to the front."

Oddly Kita felt a rare kinship with Jillian after the past few days. "Any word from Marsh?"

"No." A worried expression entered her eyes. "I tried all his numbers again."

"I wonder where he is."

"I don't know but I'm going to kill him when he gets back."

Ha-ha. But Jillian's trouble expression sobered her up. "We'll keep looking for him then."

"Yes." Jill nodded.

"How is Hannah?"

Kita had asked Alex when she first woke up and he'd reassured her that Hannah was doing fine. Kita would still like to see her but based on the dark bruise on her temple and the limp from the gouge in her foot, she thought perhaps she should wait a day so she didn't upset the already fragile woman.

"Maria is looking after her," Jill said. "I think it's been good for both of them. The safe room is a little on the small side, but the girls don't want to leave their aunt's side."

"And as far as we know, Frank Donner still doesn't have a clue?"

"No," Jill said. "One of the girls had a kid cell. Luckily I found it before we left your apartment and disabled it."

Kita hadn't even thought to check the kids for cells. Hannah had left hers in the train station, just like Kita had instructed.

"You were right," Jill said grudgingly. "We're working on the paperwork."

Kita had known that once Jill saw the abuse that Hannah suffered, she'd be on Hannah's side. The weight that had pressed on her chest eased. What a perfect ending to an awful week.

"So far Frank Donner hasn't said a word to the authorities," Jill said. "We may be in the clear."

"Good."

"Go home. Rest," Jill advised. "Take the weekend off and we'll see you on Monday."

"Sounds good."

Alex texted her. "He's out front."

"So, good news, if he screws you blind, he already knows our secrets."

"Jill!" She flushed.

Jill laughed. "Kidding. Sort of. Enjoy your weekend."

They drove off in Alex's car. They hadn't talked about the confrontation with Darla. Kita wasn't even sure she wanted to.

She was still wiped out from the benzodiazepine Darla Nichols had given her. The urge to doze off was strong but instead she rolled her head to the side and watched her partner drive. The competent, sure touch he used to navigate the streets sparked something deep within her.

When they arrived at Kita's place, he opened the door for her. Old-fashioned, outdated, and still kinda sweet. Who knew she'd be a sucker for a man opening her car door?

They rode up in the elevator without speaking. She wasn't sure what to say, how to break the suffocating weight of silence that grew with every hushed moment.

By the time the elevator arrived, she was second-guessing the tentative plan to go to his house. Maybe he'd changed his mind. Maybe she'd changed her mind. Shit, she didn't know what she was doing.

As they strode toward her apartment, several things registered. The door was open, hanging slightly crooked, the wood splintered around the handle.

She held up her hand. "Someone's here."

Before she could say more, Alex had his weapon out and at the ready. Kita's gun was still in her apartment, which was now at the very least the scene of a break-in.

"My gun was in my apartment when I left," she whispered.

Alex gestured for her to get behind him. "You're recovering."

She didn't quite think that was it, but since he'd been so sweet, she agreed. With his non-dominant hand he pushed open the door, his weapon held in the other hand with ease.

Nothing happened.

"Wait for my okay to come inside."

Sure. And then she'd wait for Mickey Mouse to start singing "It's a Small World" before she provided backup.

As soon as Alex breached the entrance, Kita followed. He was utilizing standard sweep protocol to clear each room. She trailed behind him, her horror growing with every step. Her home, her sanctuary had been trashed.

The antique tea set she'd gotten from her Vietnamese grandmother was shattered into hundreds of pieces on the hardwood floor. Her plants had been ripped from their glazed ceramic pots and tossed around the room, roots and leaves and loamy dirt littering the Oriental carpet.

Her books and CDs were strewn in a pile in front of the bookshelves. The destruction broke her already fragile heart.

Before she could caution Alex, a bear of a man barreled from her bedroom and roared, rushing Alex in a frenzied rage.

On some level she registered that while she'd taken care of Hannah, they had all dismissed Frank Donner, when he hadn't made any noise about the kids' disappearance.

"Where is she?"

She. He just wanted his punching bag. Alex had spread his legs into a ready stance and held his weapon in a two-handed sure grip. "I'm a US Deputy Marshal. Stand down."

"I know she was here," Frank accused, his face red, spittle flying from his mouth. "I put a tracker on my daughter's phone."

There was little use pretending that she hadn't been here. Kita didn't even want to get into the legality of him tracking an adult. "Hannah left the area."

"Bullshit." Frank's fists were bunched and ready to swing. "She was in this apartment at the time the train was leaving the station. I'm not stupid."

"Let's discuss this like adults." Alex was trying to reason with a crazy man. She totally appreciated his effort but she was worried that the situation was only going to escalate.

"I'm going to get that bitch," Frank vowed.

Kita had already dialed 9-1-1. She hoped the operator could hear what he was saying because she didn't want to incite more violence. They couldn't engage this guy. But as she stood there, she was thankful that Jill had followed procedure. Otherwise, Frank Donner would be at Adams-Larsen right now.

"Just like I got my *wife*."

Holy shit. Had he just confessed to killing his wife?

"What happened to your wife, Frank?" Kita asked. They needed a recording of his confession. Then perhaps Hannah wouldn't need to disappear.

"She's dead." Not an outright confession but enough for the cops to reopen the investigation. "Now I'm going to get you."

"You don't want to do this, Frank." Alex tried to reason with the guy. "Let's sit and discuss this like rational adults."

"Fuck you!" Frank Donner rushed Alex.

But in a worthy sparring move, the same one she'd tried to get Hannah to engage in the day Kita met Alex, her guy sidestepped the enraged man. For such a big man, Frank

Donner was lighter on his feet than expected. He lunged around and bent low, and instead of attacking Alex, she could see his intent. He was preparing to tackle her, going for the smaller target.

"Oh hell no," Alex growled.

Kita got ready. The room was a mess, the debris on the floor made maneuvering severely difficult, but she wasn't going to be taken down by this bully.

Bam. Bam. Bam.

The percussive sound of the shots being fired battered her eardrum.

Frank went down in a howl of pain and blood.

Her eyes widened. Alex had shot him.

"Tell 9-1-1 we need an ambulance too." His chest was heaving and his eyes were wild.

She stood frozen. Alex had just shot Frank Donner. "You…shot him."

That was certainly against the rules.

"He was a clear and present threat to your safety," Alex said fiercely. "I was protecting you."

Except Frank didn't have a weapon. The proper protocol was to convince him to back down. To talk him out of an attack.

Kita could hear the operator squawking in the background. And Frank Donner was rolling around on the floor, clutching his leg, moaning in pain.

Alex contemplated him for a second. "You'll live." He dismissed his pain and suffering with two words.

She shouldn't laugh but for some reason, his cavalier response struck her as funny. Kita began to giggle.

Me. Giggling. "Sorry," she gasped. "Not sure what's wrong."

"Delayed reaction to stress," Alex said grimly. He wasn't

happy about it, but clearly didn't feel a single drop of remorse. "But I like the sound of you laughing."

She kinda liked it too, even if it was wildly inappropriate.

"Let's get this taken care of, and then let's go home."

Home sounded fantastic.

Chapter 23

B y the time they finished with the authorities, again, the day was closing in on night. Alex drove Kita to his home, his anxiety rising the closer they got to his simple rancher.

What had seemed like a good idea hours ago now seemed silly. She was used to living in the city. So his humble suburban home would likely feel pedantic and tame compared to her fast-paced, high-energy lifestyle.

What the hell had he been thinking?

He pulled the car into the driveway and turned off the engine. The overgrown roses underneath the large picture window seemed scraggly rather than charming. The empty flower beds beneath a trio of birch trees appeared barren.

His insecurities came rushing to the forefront. What did he really have to offer her?

"Oh."

"It's not much." He shot out of the car before she could answer.

By the time he rounded the car to open her door, she was already out and peering at his unkempt bushes.

"It's overgrown," he said unnecessarily.

"These just need a little care, a little nurturing, and they'll blossom." She was stroking the leaves like she would stroke a lover.

His cock, the unruly thing, rose at the sight of her fingers lovingly caressing the plant.

But he was stuck on her words. She was a nurturer. Sure, she'd put most of her energy into plants, as evidenced by the abundance of greenery in her apartment. But if he could just convince her to take a chance on him, perhaps they could nurture each other.

"Why did you shoot him?" She continued to stroke the plant.

"Because he could have hurt you." He couldn't bear not to touch her. He threaded his fingers through her hair and held her head in his palm.

"Oh." She breathed and lifted her gaze to his.

"I figured out that blindly following the rules can have disastrous consequences." He curled his other arm around her waist and pulled him to her.

She nodded, the silk of her hair tangling in the stubble on his chin. "True."

Alex finally decided he was going to have to be the one to go out on a limb. "I've broken pretty much every personal rule I have about relationships with you."

Kita hung her head. "I'm sure. I guess I rubbed off on you."

Alex rocked her back and forth in his arms. Her cheek rested against his thudding heart. He should wait until tomorrow. Wait until she'd completely recovered from the past few days, but suddenly he couldn't delay any longer. He had to tell her how he felt. And if it backfired and blew up in his face, so be it. "Best choices I've ever made. I'm in love with you."

Kita shoved away from him. "What? That's impossible. I've been unconscious half the time we've known each other."

Alex snorted. That made his feelings even crazier. Didn't it? But he knew how he felt. "I know. But it's still true." After everything that happened over the past twenty-four hours, he might just be riding some sort of adrenaline high but it didn't mean he was crazy.

She didn't say anything, just continued to stare at him.

"I always thought I'd follow a set pattern, meet, date for a few years. That it would be gradual, easy, predictable." His heart thudded wildly, and nerves had his hands shaking. But this was too important not to say, even if he did feel like he might throw up. "But I met you and you shattered all my preconceptions."

"And that's good?" She gripped her fingers together tightly, like she was holding back from grabbing him. They were no longer touching. He hated it.

"Go figure." He wanted to grin but this was too important to treat lightly.

"You're in love with me?" Kita repeated it as a question. She wanted to skitter away from his gaze but she forced herself to boldly stare into his eyes. Her mouth went as dry as the desert and her heart stuttered in her chest. "Almost everyone I've ever loved has let me down."

"Are you saying—"

"Don't let me down." She couldn't actually say the words. The vulnerability was too raw and too fresh. But she wanted—no, needed—to tell him how she felt. The words were necessary. As elemental as breathing.

Her heart swelled at the emotion in his eyes.

"I love you." He said it.

Kita couldn't say it back. Yet.

But as if he knew her heart, he continued speaking, "I grew up in a loving family. My parents expressed their love for each other and us kids frequently. But this is different."

Kita swallowed.

"Completely different. I need you to know. Outside my family, I've never said that to a woman."

The sheer hope in her heart was difficult to ignore.

With a confession like that, how could she not bare her soul? She opened her mouth, tried, and finally the words spilled out in a rush. "Iloveyoutoo." Crazy, too fast, and yet, just right.

"I've got a garden that needs nurturing."

"I'm good at that," she murmured, her heart slowing and filling with love, so full she could burst.

"And a heart that needs tending."

"That may take a little more time." She wrapped her arms around his waist, stepped into his embrace. "My heart needs tending too."

"I can do that." Alex curled his arms around her, so tightly she couldn't escape. Not that she wanted to.

Her heart overflowed with hope. Alex pressed his lips to hers in a tender, loving kiss.

For two opposites, their attraction was absolutely wrong, and totally perfect.

THANK YOU, thank you, thank you for reading Kita and Alex's story! I hope you enjoyed reading Stalked as much as I enjoyed writing it.

Can shy, getting over major trauma Maria convince

player Dwayne that she's ready to seize the day? If you love trapped in a snowy cabin with virgin heroines and growly, protective heroes, you'll love Hunted (ALIAS #2).

p.s. Would you like to know when my next book is available? You can sign up for my new release email list/newsletter at <u>Lisa's Confidants</u> I send out newsletters two or three times a month typically filled with info on upcoming books, friend freebies, and contests I'm involved in. I will never sell or distribute your email to other people.

p.p.s. Want to know why Sergei Polzin was really in the ALIAS offices? Check out Never Say Never (book 2 in my Nostradamus Prophecies series)....

p.p.p.s. If you did enjoy this novel, below are a few ways you can help a writer out!!

Good: Lend the book to a friend

Better: Recommend the book to your friends

Best: Leave a review at Amazon, BN, iBooks, Kobo, Google Play, Goodreads...basically any place they sell or review eBooks. Every review helps my work get out to other readers and I cannot even express how much it means to me when you let people know you liked my work. Readers have so many choices nowadays and limited dollars to spend. It can be difficult to take a chance on a new author even if the premise sounds appealing. By reviewing books, you give other readers insight into the story world and help them make informed purchases.

Thank you, thank you, thank you for your support!!

Also by Lisa Hughey

Black Cipher Files Romantic Suspense

The Encounter, A Prequel to Blowback

Blowback

Betrayals

Burned

Dangerous Game

**These books are also available in paperback

Black Cipher Files Box Set (includes Blowback, Betrayals, and Burned)

Snow Creek Christmas

Love on Main Street: A Snow Creek Christmas – 7 Author anthology

One Silent Night (from Love on Main Street)

Miracle on Main Street (standalone novella)

Family Stone Romantic Suspense

Stone Cold Heart, (Jess, Family Stone #1)

Carved in Stone (Connor, Family Stone #2)

Heart of Stone (Riley, Family Stone #3)

Still the One (Jack, Family Stone #4)

Jar of Hearts (Keisha & Shane, Family Stone #5)

Queen of Hearts (Shelley, Family Stone #6)

Author's Note

I've had the idea for Adams-Larsen in my head for a long time. Years ago, I went to a presentation by a man who helps people disappear. It was fascinating and started the seed for the ALIAS books. Then I read a book about the US Marshals' Witness Security program and according to the author one of the biggest problems they had was relocating people who were witnesses but not criminals. So I married the two ideas together and ALIAS was born.

I hope you enjoyed the first book in this series. Next up will be Maria and Dwayne's story. Maria is finally getting her Happy Ever After!

About Lisa

USA Today Bestselling Author Lisa Hughey started writing romance in the fourth grade. That particular story involved a prince and an engagement. Now, she writes about strong heroines who are perfectly capable of rescuing themselves and the heroes who love both their strength and their vulnerability. She pens romances of all types—suspense, paranormal, and contemporary—but at their heart, all her books celebrate the power of love.

She lives in Cape Ann Massachusetts with her fabulously supportive husband, two out of three awesome mostly-grown kids, and one somewhat grumpy cat.

Beach walks, hiking, and traveling are her favorite ways to pass the time when she isn't plotting new ways to get her characters to fall in love.

Lisa loves to hear from readers and has tons of places you can connect with her. It's a wonder she gets any writing done at all....

Sign Up for Lisa's Confidants
  Visit Lisa on the Web

Follow Lisa's Boards on Pinterest
Follow Lisa on Instagram
Email Lisa
Be Lisa's Friend on Goodreads
Like Lisa on Facebook at Lisa Hughey: My Books

Excerpt of Stone Cold Heart

Want to read where it all started? Here's an excerpt of
Stone Cold Heart, the first book in the Family Stone series.
This book is free at all retailers.

Family Stone #1 Jess

In the early evening dusk, Jess Stone lay on her stomach in
the twenty-foot-high rubble of a demolished church,
underneath a black and gray city-scape tarp intended to
camouflage her position. A sharp-edged chunk of debris
dug into her lower rib cage, the scope of the Remington
M24 cool and familiar against her face.

Her standard uniform of jeans, running shoes, and plain
black t-shirt rendered her just another anonymous and
transient relief worker...which she was actually. A black
baseball cap hid her distinctive multi-hued blonde hair. The
paper mask kept out the contaminated dust from the
destroyed buildings but did little to stem the overwhelming
stench of decaying bodies.

Tanks rumbled through the destroyed coastal town, their
public address system blasting warnings for citizens to stay

in their homes, curfew was in effect. The threat was a joke. Ninety percent of the people in the town didn't have homes left. Those who did were terrified to go back inside. In the fetid, humidity choked air, the tent cities erected in the parks and on the beach were seething masses of the injured and shock struck.

The substandard construction in the small country had never been enough to withstand the angry might of Mother Nature. Buildings had toppled like a stack of Tinkertoys, and left crumbling cement walls with twisted rebar poking out of the jagged ruins like a skeletal hand.

Trapped in the concrete pieces that littered the ground, the heat from the tropical day seared through her thin sturdy clothing. The stank of the raw sewage that ran in rivulets through the streets overpowered the salt-laden breeze off the ocean. People, covered with the grit of pulverized buildings and humans, shuffled along with blank vacant stares. Two weeks after the quake, still in shock, their lives decimated first by nature and then kicked and beaten by the ineffectiveness of a flawed relief system. Hundreds of humanitarian agencies had descended on the population duplicating efforts and yet completely missing the need in other areas. The government was ostensibly trying to coordinate the effort, however the mass chaos was undeniable.

Through the Leupold Ultra M3 fixed power sight, she tracked the movements of Henri LeRoy, leader of this tiny island nation, violator of human rights and dignity, and all around poor excuse for a human being.

Sickness roiled in her stomach. The power bar she'd eaten for breakfast threatened to add to the rubble pile as she tried to figure out how in the hell she'd ended up here.

Back behind a sniper rifle with the power over life and death trembling in the muscles of her right trigger finger.

Dammit. When she'd decided to take control of her life and quit the FBI, she hadn't wanted to do this anymore.

She'd wanted to be a simple relief worker. She'd wanted to connect with her family, brothers and mother.

But that bitch, fate, had slapped her upside the head and now here she was, where she'd sworn she never wanted to be again. Looking through the scope of a high-powered rifle, with a crystal clear head shot and a murky sense of right and wrong.

With little fanfare, she could blast LeRoy's brain matter all over the silk-covered walls and the antique Louis the XIV scrolled chairs in the receiving room of his ridiculously elegant weekend mansion which, since built properly, had sustained minimal damage. Her muscles twitched with the knowledge and acceptance that with one slow slide of her finger, the despotic, amoral leader would be history.

Jess didn't want to kill him, didn't want to be directly responsible for another death. She didn't want this choice. She'd given up this kind of life. She'd left the FBI after a series of high stress cases to get away from the doubt and guilt that had crippled her. To make her own decisions about right and wrong rather than carry out the commands of her bosses.

But if Henri LeRoy lived, chances were astronomical that many other citizens would die.

And yeah, she'd probably been manipulated into this. Actually no probably about it. Assassination had not been listed as one of her duties when she'd joined Global Humanitarian Relief. Damn her brother anyway.

But now all she could do was lay here in the desecrated

remains of the former church and hope that her special skill set wouldn't be needed.

Fortunately, she was secondary backup.

And unless several things went horribly wrong, she would break down her weapon, get back to the relief aid encampment, back to actually helping people, and be out of here without ever firing her rifle.

Then she could hand out seed packets to her heart's content and figure out what she was going to do next. If she'd stay with GHR and her brothers, or go. First, she had to get through the next two hours.

But if something did go wrong...she prayed that if she was called upon, she could make the right decision. Make the shot. Cold zero.

Acknowledgments

To all my usual suspects:

Thanks to Adrienne Bell and LGC Smith for your continued support and our coffee klatching.

Thanks to the Pens Fatales for seven years of writing and friendship.

Thanks to Deb Nemeth, my fabulous editor, for helping me fine tune and articulate Kita and Alex's story.

Thanks to Chelsea, my assistant, who picks up the slack and calmly handles anything I ask of her.

Many thanks to Robin Ludwig at http:// gobookcoverdesign.com/ for her beautiful cover design. It was a pleasure to work with her!

And finally, thank you to the readers who continue to buy my work and leave me such lovely reviews. I cannot express how much I appreciate every single one of you!